D0115915

WITHDRAWN

WINNIPEG
JAN 26 2017 ✓
PUBLIC LIBRARY

LiFE OF ZARF

TROLL
OVERBOARD

LIFE OF ZARF

TROLL OVERBOARD

ROB
HARRELL

DIAL BOOKS *for*
YOUNG READERS

DIAL BOOKS FOR YOUNG READERS

Penguin Young Readers Group • An imprint of Penguin Random House LLC

375 Hudson Street • New York, New York 10014

Copyright © 2016 by Rob Harrell

Penguin supports copyright. Copyright fuels creativity, encourages diverse voices, promotes free speech, and creates a vibrant culture. Thank you for buying an authorized edition of this book and for complying with copyright laws by not reproducing, scanning, or distributing any part of it in any form without permission. You are supporting writers and allowing Penguin to continue to publish books for every reader.

Library of Congress Cataloging-in-Publication Data

Names: Harrell, Rob, author, illustrator.

Title: Troll overboard / by Rob Harrell.

Description: New York, NY : Dial Books for Young Readers, an imprint of Penguin Random House LLC, [2016] | Series: Life of Zarf; 3 | Sequel to: Troll who cried wolf. | Summary: "Prince Roquefort's quest for magical, height-increasing beans leads Zarf and his friends on a high-seas adventure, where they meet sea monsters, pirates, and a mer-pig"—Provided by publisher.

Identifiers: LCCN 2015049505 | ISBN 9780803741058 (hardcover)

Subjects: | CYAC: Trolls—Fiction. | Adventure and adventurers—Fiction. | Humorous stories.

Classification: LCC PZ7.H2348 Tn 2016 | DDC [Fic]—dc23 LC record available at https://lccn.loc.gov/2015049505

1 3 5 7 9 10 8 6 4 2

Printed in the United States of America

Designed by Jason Henry • Text set in Italian Old Style MT Std

For all the trolls out there

LiFE OF ZARF

TROLL
OVERBOARD

· 1 ·

A ROUGH START

How did I end up here?

I was making my way along a thin ledge on the Dumpty Cliffs, gasping for breath and trying to ignore the two-hundred-foot drop to the rock-filled waves below. My shoulder kept grazing the rough wall as my paws scrambled to find an exposed root or something to hang on to.

Then there was the growling. I didn't dare look back, but it was getting louder. That growl was packed full of anger and hatred and quite a bit of drool . . . wolf drool, to be specific.

I turned a sharp corner, and there—I don't know how—was Prince Roquefort. As much as I can't stand that little waste of oxygen, I was so happy to see him, I could have kissed him.

Okay, not kissed—but maybe a high five or a firm handshake. You get the idea.

Roquefort reached out with his stubby little gloved hand.

I grabbed his hand just as the ledge gave way under my paws, and I was suddenly hanging on to the prince for dear life. I heard the rocks falling and bouncing off of the cliff below me.

A mean little grin spread across Roquefort's face. "Wow, troll. You're even stupider than you look—which is really saying something!" He let out an insulting snort. "Have a nice fall!"

He threw his head back and started laughing his stupid hyena laugh as he relaxed his hand and let go.

Terror shot through me as I flipped backward into thin air. Time slowed down like a slow-motion replay.

There were some huge, bone-breaking boulders down there, but I was thinking I had a small chance of missing them . . . when something burst out of the water.

A shark. A gigantic jumping-through-the-air Shark Week shark—and I was headed right for it.

It was opening its mouth, revealing row after row of enormous teeth, when something burst forward from its throat.

It was a huge, snarling Snuffweasel, its fur matted with seawater and shark spit, its fangs gnashing and waiting to tear into me.

The weasel opened its mouth wider and wider . . . and then something burst out of *its* mouth.

That's when I started screaming. It was the Big Bad Wolf, licking his big, gnarly-looking chops. He grinned up at me and spoke in a low growl.

PERFECT TIMING. I WAS FEELING A BIT *SNACKY.*

I was three feet away as he opened his mouth impossibly wide. Then two feet away. Then I was sitting up in my bed screaming my lungs out into my dark bedroom.

I gasped as I realized I was awake. I frantically felt my legs and arms to make sure they were still attached. I heard heavy paws pounding down the hall as I sat there gulping air, my heart trying to slam its way out of my rib cage. My parents burst into the room.

I swallowed hard. "I'm okay. I'm fine. Just another . . . You know."

Some of the tension came out of my mom's shoulders as she sat down beside me. "Poor guy. I'm sure these things will fade away at some point."

She put her paw on my shoulder—and quickly pulled it away. "Oh, you're soaked."

She reached back and felt my soggy pillow. "Why don't you jump in the shower and I'll change these sheets."

(I'd like to make it perfectly clear that my sheets were soaked with SWEAT. I did NOT—I repeat, NOT—wet the bed. The last thing I need is any misinformation going around at school.)

I stood in the hot shower as the last of the shivers left my body. This was getting to be a habit. I'd been having night terrors almost nightly since our run-in with Big Bad. I hadn't told Chester or Kevin about them. I just wasn't ready to say anything—and Kevin was enough of a worry-factory without throwing this in the mix.

I dried off and put on fresh clothes my mom had set by the sink. When I walked into the bedroom, my dad was sitting on the edge of my freshly made bed.

I nodded as he stood up and held back the covers for me. I climbed in and he started tucking me in like he used to when I was little.

"These things'll pass, Zarf. It's just your brain working out some of the stuff you've been through." He stepped back and put his hands on his hips. "But if you ever want to talk about it . . ."

I smiled weakly. "Thanks."

RIGHT, THEN. SLEEP TIGHT.

He ruffled my hair and walked to the door. Then he turned. "And . . . you know I'd be there tomorrow if there was any way, right? It's just . . . work. My boss . . ."

"I know you would, Dad. I understand."

He gave me a crooked smile as an enormous snore echoed down the hall. I laughed.

My dad laughed back. *"Nothing* wakes your gramps." Then he flipped off the light.

Let me explain a bit, for any newbies.

My name is Zarf Belford and I'm a troll. An Eastern Prairie Troll, if you're into genealogy. I live with my parents and my gramps in a house under the Carousel Street Bridge. In the Village of Cotswin, in the Kingdom of Notswin.

I am—largely because of my smellier, furrier, floppy-eared traits—pretty much the lowest class of student at Cotswin Middle School. You may be thinking: "But, puppies are smelly, furry, and have floppy ears, and everyone loves them!" Well, trust me. It doesn't carry over to trolls. I'm pretty used to it.

I get by, though. Big thanks go to my two best friends, Kevin and Chester, for helping me stay sane.

KEVIN LITTLEPIG
- OLYMPIC-LEVEL WORRIER
- GOES SERIOUSLY BONKERS OVER ANY AND ALL MUTTON-RELATED PRODUCTS

CHESTER FLINTWATER
- SON OF THE ROYAL COURT JESTER
- NOT FUNNY
- KNOWS 4,000 KNOCK-KNOCK JOKES (UNFORTUNATELY)

Okay. That's all you get for now. The rest you'll figure out as we go.

I woke up that next morning and counted my lucky stars that I hadn't had another wolf dream after my midnight freak-out. Then I remembered it was Career Day.

Every Friday that month, Mr. Hirsch (period three: Fable Studies) was having three parents come in to tell our class about what they do for a living. Today was supposed to be my dad's visit, but his boss had decided at the last minute that he wasn't giving him the time off. Now I was going to have to explain to the class that not only was my dad a *mog diver,* but he was also low enough on the totem pole that he couldn't take the day off.

I am in no way embarrassed by my dad. He's the

hardest-working mog diver in the kingdom—as was my gramps before him. But mog diving isn't exactly a glamorous job. (Mog is the stuff they use to make pencil erasers.)

It's common knowledge that trolls aren't the sharpest swords in the arsenal, so mog diving is a pretty common troll job. And we're not exactly first pick for upper management jobs within the company either.

I was thinking about all of this while I pushed some scrambled Swampfrog eggs around on my plate.

But that all left my mind when Kevin showed up. I almost didn't hear his weak little knock at the door, and when I opened it, he looked like a Weepy Gnome after a viewing of *Old Yeller*. He was snorting and wiping his eyes and looked like he could barely hold his head up.

I pulled him inside. My mom had some extra Mutton-Tarts I thought might fix whatever was ailing him. "Who's gone, Kev?"

Kevin seemed to crumple as he buried his face in his hooves. "MEREDITH THE MEAT GIRL!!" He was really sobbing now.

Kevin had once held hands (and hooves) with the butcher's daughter Meredith after a group of us went to a movie. They held hands for about two minutes, that is, but Kevin had talked about it ever since as if theirs was one of the great breathless romances of all time.

I ducked into the kitchen and brought out a handful of Mutton-Tarts. Kevin turned away, insulted. "My heart is broken, Zarf. I can't even think about food."

Then I guess he caught a whiff of them. He slowly looked back over his shoulder, sniffling.

He snuffled out an explanation about how Meredith had sent him a "Let's just be friends" text that morning.

NOOOOO!!

I spent the walk to school trying to console him, but the poor little guy was really beside himself. A couple of times he had to stop and bend over like he'd been punched in the gut.

OH, LORDY!! THE PAIN! IT COMES IN WAVES!!

Chester met us at the edge of the ball field and tried to help out—in typical Chester fashion.

"You'll be okay, Kev. I um . . ." You could tell he was really trying to find the right thing to say. "Did you hear why the gnome broke up with his girlfriend at the gym?"

Kevin just wiped his snout and glared at Chester.

Kevin groaned, put his head down, and shuffled into the school. I gave Chester a "Really?" look and we walked in together. Chester looked baffled.

"I just thought a funny joke might help!"

"Yeah!" I gave him a sideways glance. "A funny one might have!"

· 2 ·

NEVER
EASY

TROLLS EAT BOOGERS

RELATIVELY TAME TODAY.

I threw some stuff in my locker and scrubbed the graffiti off of the door. It wasn't the first time this had happened—by a long shot—so I kept some cleaner and a rag on the top shelf.

I was making my way to class when I turned the corner and saw Rebb Glumfort, one of our weirder wizard students, pinned against the wall by one of Prince Roquefort's bodyguard ogres. Roquefort was peppering him with questions, and I overheard a bit of what Rebb was saying as I approached.

"They're very effective, b-but they're all gone!" Rebb was having a hard time getting the words out. "Th-they were taken way out—on Royal Orders!—and thrown into the deep . . ."

Without thinking, I shoved the ogre—a shove fueled by more than a little troll anger—hard enough that he stumbled and Rebb slid to the floor. Rebb clutched his throat and took off running for the wizard wing, his robe fluttering behind him.

Prince Roquefort spun on me, enraged. "WHAT WAS *THAT*??"

I was opening my mouth to tear into him when the bell rang. We both turned and ran for Miss Flett's classroom, pushing and shoving and trying to trip each other as we went. I'm not sure where the ogre went. Bullying 101, maybe.

Have I made it clear that Prince Roquefort is my least favorite person on earth? Scratch that. He's my least favorite living thing on earth. I'd rather deal with a grumpy Slaughterbeast.

Roquefort shot me a nasty look as we settled into our desks. He mouthed something that looked like "You're dead, troll." (It also looked like "Horse head roll," but that doesn't make any sense, so I'm sticking with the first one.)

I turned the other way and saw Sierra smiling and giving me a "Calm down" gesture.

Sierra Scarlet. We'd been through a whole showdown with the Big Bad Wolf recently—after it turned out she was the daughter of Red Ridinghood.

Red had fled the kingdom years ago, distancing herself from Sierra to keep her safe from the wolves. (We saw how well that worked out.) Anyway . . . long story. Nobody knew if Red was still alive, and she hadn't returned to Notswin as of yet, so Sierra lived with her aunt.

I felt a blush spread across my face. I really hated when my troll blood and anger got the better of me—and having Sierra see it made me feel like swamp mud. We'd been hanging out more lately, but I didn't really think we were a couple or anything. Right? I'm not sure how you know when . . . I'm not . . . Stop bugging me about it!!

I took a deep breath and settled in as Miss Flett blew into the room. The class went by fairly smoothly—except for a few death glares from Prince Fabulousness.

I was heading down the hall to Mr. Hirsch's class, dreading telling him that my dad was a no-show, when I noticed a familiar shock of gray, wiry hair towering over the crowd.

Gramps was leaning against the wall outside the door to my class.

I was shocked. "What are you doing here?"

"Well, I used ta be a pretty good mog diver m'self, ya know." He straightened up and raised an eyebrow like he was all fancy. "An' I couldn't leave ya hangin'. Not yer fault yer da's boss is a twit."

I was so relieved. "Thanks, Gramps." I gave him a quick hug and heard a snort-laugh from Prince Roquefort as he slipped into the room behind me.

Gramps seemed excited. "I spoke wi' yer teacher, 'n' he's fine with me fillin' in. There's a coupla parents talkin' before me."

He leaned down and nudged me with his huge elbow.

HOPE THEY DON'T HAVE MORE EXCITIN' JOBS THAN ME 'N'YER POPS, Y'KNOW?

Famous last words.

The first parent up was the Royal Candy Maker (Kent Wilshoom's mom), who came loaded with huge bags of magical candies for each student in the class. Goo-Zoo Blasters. Fazzle Bars. Splash-whizzies. You name it.

I MEAN, REALLY??

As she left the room, I slid lower in my seat hoping the next parent would have a boring and/or disgusting job.

The next parent was the king.

HEAD OF
THE CLASS

GREETINGS,
LOYAL SUBJECTS!

I like King Cheznott. He's a good king and all. But this was kind of obnoxious. He was literally played into the room by a Royal Trumpeter. He had an attendant who walked in front of him sprinkling rose petals on the ground.

They couldn't have saved the king for last??

Even more annoying was the way Prince Roquefort glowed as the king entered. He looked like his head was about to burst from all the pride.

I wish it had.

The king had barely started speaking before Roquefort began throwing out requests.

Excuse me if I don't go into all the details, but it went on for a while and everyone was thoroughly dazzled. Enormous jewels were shown. The Royal Prancing Equestrian Team was paraded through the room at one point, accompanied by twirling acrobats.

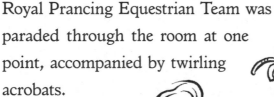

In a word, it was a disaster. The sounds of the trumpets and horse hooves were still echoing down the hall as Mr. Hirsch introduced Gramps. I considered jumping out the window.

Gramps strolled in like nothing out of the ordinary had just happened.

WHA'S UP, LADS 'N' LASSES? I'M ZARF'S GRANDDA.

There was empty silence until Roquefort piped up.

MR. HIRSCH? CAN I GO TO THE BATHROOM WHILE THE OLD TROLL TALKS?

Gramps didn't wait for Mr. Hirsch to respond. "What yeh can do is shut yer tongue hole 'n' behave, ya little turd."

The whole class froze, including Mr. Hirsch.

The prince nearly fell out of his chair. "What did you say to me, troll??"

Mr. Hirsch snapped out of it and stepped up to Gramps, whispering into his ear. Gramps listened before speaking to Hirsch in a low voice that we all still heard. "But, he is. I mean, we all know it. He's not worth the paper 'e wipes his—"

Mr. Hirsch cut him off. Gramps just shrugged his big shoulders and went on.

"All righ'. Whatever. I'm here ta tell yeh 'bout mog divin'."

There was a low groan from the class, and I couldn't completely blame them. But as my gramps started in about all the years he'd spent as a diver, something else happened. Something completely unexpected.

Suddenly Prince Roquefort was fascinated. Like, leaning-forward-on-his-desk, eyes-wide-open into it.

Gramps sighed as he looked over at him. "Yes. I did."

The prince looked like he could barely contain himself. "And you know how to drive a boat? You know how to read maps and use compasses and stuff like that?"

Gramps cleared his throat and stared at the prince for a long moment. "Yes, lad. Tha's what I'm sayin'."

He went on. I'm pretty sure the rest of the class went on autopilot at this point, but Roquefort hung on every word my gramps said. Now . . . I'm suspicious of everything that kid does—so my first thought was that he was messing with us—but as gramps went on, he sure seemed excited about the diving life.

Some kids like dinosaurs, some like robots, some like horses. Seemed like the prince's thing was the ocean. Who knew?

After class, the prince made a beeline for my gramps. When I hurried over to see what he was up to, he turned to me excitedly.

"Oh, hey Zarf! Sorry about all that business before."

I WAS JUST HAVIN' SOME YUKS WITH YOU, YA BIG LUG!

PUNCH

Gross! This chummy, sincere version of Roquefort was sending up red flags in my brain—and making my skin crawl. He turned back to Gramps.

"I had no idea your family were mog divers! I've always been *fascinated* by diving—since I was a little prince-in-training!"

Gramps and I were both staring at him with the same blank look.

"Seriously!! I know that sounds weird, but as the Royal Offspring, I live a terribly sheltered life. I've always wanted to go out on a boat." Then his eyes went wide like Kevin at a Mutton Festival. "OH! Could we go out on a boat?? Could you take us, sir?? Maybe tomorrow?? I'd just be so super-duper honored, I wouldn't know what to do with myself!"

I think it was the "sir" that got to Gramps. He's pretty smart as far as trolls go, but he's not immune to flattery. He chuckled.

WELL, I...I MEAN, IF IT MEANS THA' MUCH TO YEH. MAYBE I COULD...

I shot him a big "What the heck are you doing??" look, but I could see that Gramps was already lost in the thought of a day at sea. He had that faraway look in his eyes, like when he tells his old diving stories.

The prince started clapping his little hands excitedly. "Oh goodie! Yes! Can I bring a friend?"

HE HAS A FRIEND?

Gramps was sold. "Why not? An' Zarf'll come along too."

The smile on Roquefort's face faded—just for a moment, but I saw it. Then that thousand-watt smile was back.

Gramps told him to meet us at six a.m. at the harbor, and the prince ran off like it was the night before Christmas. I looked up at Gramps as he watched him go.

"You know he's not on the up-and-up, right?"

Gramps laughed. "I wouldn't trust tha' li'l weasel any further'n a gnome hop."

"Maybe some fresh air 'n' hard work'll do th' little snot some good."

· 4 ·

SOMETHING
FISHY

Kevin was in full meltdown mode at lunch. Sierra was listening patiently and rubbing his back. We got a little worried when he wouldn't eat, so I got our lunch lady and good friend Goldie Locks to whip him up a little mutton pudding.

"Maybe a wet willie or two."

The pudding helped—a little. Rebb came over and put a quick Soothing Spell on Kev. Then he thanked me for interfering in the hall earlier.

The Soothing Spell started to calm Kev down and I was about to bring up the prince's new nautical fascination when the bell rang.

We all agreed to head to the tree house after last period.

The very first signs of fall were arriving, and the Wishing Tree was freaking out about losing his leaves (as he did every year).

I pulled out a jar of peanut butter and fed some to the tree to keep him occupied and quiet. I had some things to discuss.

Kevin seemed calmer, and maybe a bit woozy from Rebb's Soothing Spell.

IT'S ALL GOOD. EVERYTHING'S GRAVY.

Sierra had brought a few cans of Flumpfruit Splash from her aunt's house. As we cracked those open, I told them all about the prince's sudden interest in mog diving.

Sierra took a sip and looked off over the hills, thinking. "Well, bottom line, he's up to something."

I MEAN, HE'S **ALWAYS** UP TO SOMETHING.

"Right??" I was getting worked up again. "But what? I mean, he seemed genuinely excited. I don't think that part was an act."

Chester was fiddling with one of the bells on his jester hat and mumbling to himself. "Rotten little over-cologned, no-good . . ."

Kev looked like he had something to add, but the thought faded away and he flopped back on the tree house floor.

Might need to tell Rebb to give him a half-spell next time.

Chester launched into a long story about his fifth-period gym class. He'd forgotten his gym clothes and was forced to suffer through volleyball wearing a pair of Mr. Lump's enormous shorts.

We were all laughing—Sierra snorted so loud, it startled the Wishing Tree—except for poor Kev, who could barely keep his eyes open.

Just before he nodded off, I got the three of them to agree to go along on the big boat ride. Chester seemed especially into it.

I started to groan when Sierra's phone rang. She pulled it out and checked the caller ID. "It's my aunt."

You could see her brace herself as she answered—

and suddenly we could all hear her aunt's shrill voice screeching from the other end. Sierra actually had to hold the phone away from her ear.

YES, MA'AM. OF COURSE, AUNT ROSE.

She hung up and started zipping her bag, chewing at her bottom lip like she does when something's bothering her. "I've gotta go. I forgot I had a Finishing Class this afternoon." She rolled her eyes and started down the rope ladder.

"Finishing what?" Chester asked, letting out a fairly impressive belch.

"It's a class to turn me into a proper young lady." Sierra hopped the rest of the way to the ground.

PSSSH. GOOD LUCK WITH *THAT!*

Sierra chuckled, stuck her tongue out at me, and gave a sarcastic curtsy. "I'll see you gentlemen at the boat. I need to go get 'finished.'"

That night, my dad and I helped Gramps organize the supplies we'd need for the dive. My dad apologized all over himself that he couldn't come—mog diving is a seven-days-a-week job—while Gramps squeezed into his old diving suit to make sure it still fit.

Not exactly. My dad ran off to borrow an XXXL suit from a friend while my mom and I worked to slice the old one off Gramps before it cut off his circulation. I was looking for a second pair of scissors when my phone lit up. It was Sierra.

Bad new, Z. Can't make it tomorrow.

WHAAA? Why??

Sorry. Auntie is NOT happy with me. Guess I'm "not taking my finishing seriously."

That lady "seriously" needs to relax.

Tell me about it. She needs a blast of Rebb's Soothing Spell.

Okay. Well...Have fun with your delightful aunt. Maybe I'll bring you a big lump of mog.

Sigh. A girl can dream.

· 5 ·

HARBOR
DAY

OH, THIS IS HORRIBLE. WE'RE GONNA DROWN OR GET PECKED BY SEAGULLS OR...

Gramps and I picked up an unhappy Kevin on the way to the harbor. He felt it was unfair that he'd been roped into this trip while under the influence. "That little wizard Rebb gave me a temporary lobotomy!!"

Kevin was loaded down with a bracelet, necklace, and three or four patches, all designed to prevent seasickness.

He wasn't letting up. "Do they make a sunblock higher than three hundred SPF? If I get too much sun, I start to look like a football."

We were walking up to the harbormaster's office when Chester arrived. He pounced out of the bushes wearing a full pirate costume and waving a little wooden sword.

Gramps just shook his head and knocked on the weathered office door.

Chester was all kinds of jazzed up. "I've always wanted to be a pirate! Like Jack Sparrow or Redbeard the Unapproachable. They're so cool!" He got into his joke-telling stance. "Do you know where pirates get their tattoos?" He looked around at us, a huge expectant grin on his face.

The office door creaked open, and standing there was the skinniest, oldest living man I'd ever seen. His scraggly beard looked like it had bits of porridge and fishing line in it. He was sporting a stretched-out pair of dingy red long johns.

Gramps lit up. "Jack Sprat, ya old dog! How are yeh? How's tha' lovely wife a' yours?"

Sprat looked us all over. "She's fine. Likes the sweets a bit too much, but you know that." He spit into his fist and wiped it on his long johns before breaking into a startling, mostly toothless grin. He gave Gramps an exaggerated handshake before going in for the hug. "How ya been, Belford, ya old bilge flinger?"

I wasn't sure what a bilge flinger was—or sure that I wanted to know. They carried on for a few minutes before Gramps reminded him he needed to borrow a boat.

"Right, right, right! I'm gettin' sketchy upstairs these days." He tapped his head. "I got a beauty for ya. Pick o' the litter."

He turned and was locking up the office when the prince and a huge ogre bodyguard came around the corner.

If Chester looked ridiculous, Roquefort looked insane. He was fully decked out in old-timey naval finery. I tried to stifle a laugh, but couldn't.

Harbormaster Sprat stood there sucking on one of his few remaining teeth and looking the prince up and down before giving a sarcastic salute.

Sprat let out a wheezy laugh as we followed him down the dock, giving us pointers in his raspy voice.

"You boys listen to every word this ol' troll here tells ya, right? 'E's one a' the best mog divers this kingdom's e'er seen."

I looked over at Gramps. He looked back and waggled his eyebrows at me. Sprat went on as two gnomes walked past us struggling to carry a lobster trap twice their size.

"Now, the sea ain't no place fer horseplay. There's *real* pirates out there." He turned his squinty eye on Chester. "One misstep and you can end up in trouble. That's how ships get lost in th' dreaded Berundi Rectangle. Or smashed against th' rocks."

OR ON TH' OCEAN FLOOR.

I heard Kevin swallow loudly beside me.

Suddenly Sprat stopped and turned. "An' you all know about Ol' Lady Seaweed an' her offspring, right?"

The prince let out a rude laugh.

THE SEA WITCH? SHE'S A MYTH.

Sprat stopped. Suddenly he was right in the prince's face. "Like mud, she is. She's as real as this scar, ya chubby little turnip." Sprat pointed a crooked finger at a bumpy scar that nearly circled his throat.

NEAR TOOK MY HEAD OFF, THAT MYTH DID.

"Big as a dragon and twice as nasty, she is."

I heard a flump and realized Kevin had passed out on the wooden planks beside me.

Then, just as suddenly, Sprat straightened back up. "Anyhow, you prob'ly won't see her. And here we are! Slip 96-Z." We all turned and looked at the boat. At least, I guess you'd call it a boat. My first thought was, Floating Pile of Scrap Wood.

It had the shape of a boat, but barely. Paint was chipping off every warped, weather-beaten board. There were barnacles and what looked like oyster shells growing on the hull at the waterline. The name was so faded you could barely make it out. *Once Upon a Brine.*

Kevin groaned as he came to. Then he took one look at the boat and passed right back out.

The prince was outraged. "We're going on . . . on THAT?? Do you have any idea who I am??"

Sprat spit in his fist again. "I do, Yer Highness. I do, indeed. An' she's a fine vessel."

Roquefort stood there sputtering and making exasperated noises until Gramps stepped forward. He shook Sprat's hand and smiled. "It's perfect, Jack. Absolutely perfect."

The prince continued to stomp around in a huff.

Before he walked away, Sprat leaned in and spoke to my gramps. I barely heard him over the prince's complaining. "Make sure ya have these kids back in a coupla hours. There's a storm comin' this afternoon, an' not a nice one, at that."

· ANCHORS
AWEIGH

We pulled away from the dock just after seven a.m., with my gramps at the wheel, singing a series of off-color sea chanteys that probably shouldn't be repeated here.

As we left the harbor, I stood at the back of the ship, smelling the ocean air and watching our village grow smaller. I'd never realized just how picturesque it was, and a feeling of peace and calm washed over me. For about a second.

Now that we were on the water, the prince was peppering Gramps with a stream of questions. "How do you steer? Where are we going? Can you show me on a map? Does the compass tell you how to get there? How do you use a compass?" Roquefort's ogre stood by glaring at Kevin and Chester and me in a way that was making my troll senses send up flares.

Kevin suddenly spun around and bolted for the railing, yelling, "I'm gonna boot!!" He got there just in time, and I grabbed on to a hoof so he wouldn't end up overboard.

Chester patted him gently on the back. "Atta boy. Get the bad stuff out and you'll have your sea legs in no time."

We stood there listening to the poor guy turn himself inside out for a few minutes before Chester spoke again.

"You know what sound pirates make after drinking bad rum?"

I shot him a stern "Not now" look.

Eventually, Kevin's Dramamine kicked in. He hunkered down in the back of the boat looking dazed but less green. Chester grabbed him a bottle of water out of the cooler as I went up to check in on Gramps and Roquefort.

The lesson was still in full swing. I walked up as Roquefort was asking about the Berundi Rectangle.

"Which way is it? Can you show me?"

Gramps looked at the prince like he'd grown two more heads.

"Are yeh soft in the head, boy? Yeh don' wanna go near there if yeh value yer life. Unless you'd *enjoy* dyin' in th' belly of a sea beast."

The prince wasn't deterred.

RIGHT, RIGHT.

"I get that. But if you show me, then I can be sure I don't go near it!"

Gramps stared at him. "Yeh don' need ta worry about it. It's way out here." He stabbed a huge finger at the parchment map the prince was holding.

The prince grabbed a pencil from behind his ear and circled the spot Gramps had indicated. "So, right here??" He looked way too eager.

Gramps rolled his eyes. "Wha'ever. Yeah. Tha's where it is. But it's a couple hours past where we're goin'."

Chester walked up. "So! Grampsy! Whattaya got on this thing? Couple of Elven-rude 660s back there?"

Gramps looked surprised. "Ya know boat engines? I thought you was jus' the comic relief."

Chester sniffed and leaned against the railing.

Roquefort made a scoffing noise. "Pssh. You probably googled that just now."

Chester looked hurt. "I did not."

Gramps chuckled. "Not likely, Yer Princeness. There'll be no Internettin' today. There's no reception once yeh get past th' breakers." He closed his eyes and took a long sniff of the salty air.

JUST US AN' THE SEA NOW, LADS.

Somehow, Kevin heard all of that over the engines. "No phones?!?! Oh, no no no!"

WE'RE ALL GONNA DIE SALT-WATERY FISH-RELATED DEATHS!!

Thirty minutes later, Gramps cut the engine. He looked over at the prince's guard. "Hey, um . . . ogre. What's your name?"

"Course it is. Can yeh throw the anchor over th' side, Trunk?"

Without a word, Trunk walked over and tossed the enormous thing into the water like it weighed nothing.

Gramps turned to us all and put his paws on his hips.

The prince started jumping up and down. "OH!! Oh, will you show us how it's done??!?"

Gramps glared at Roquefort until he settled down. "If I can continue . . . The first thing tha's gonna happen is I'm gonna suit up 'n' show you the drill while you watch. M'kay?"

The prince rolled his eyes and gave a sarcastic little snort. What was that about? I thought he was all sea-happy.

I helped Gramps into his huge suit as Kevin paced the length of the deck, muttering.

"Oh, this is awful. You can barely see land from here! And the sky's getting dark over that way!"

Gramps quieted him down and started explaining his diving helmet.

"So this hose that comes out th' top? Tha's what I breathe through. Any prankster decides to plug it up or drop their gum in there as a joke, I'll come up 'n' pound yeh into weak porridge, 'kay?" His eyebrow shot up as he gave Roquefort and his ogre a pointed look.

I helped Gramps fit the helmet over his head and ears and seal it to the suit. He looked like one of those diver figures people put in their goldfish bowl.

(MURMUR MURMUR MUFFLED SOMETHING.)

He said something, but it was kind of hard to hear through the helmet—so we all smiled and gave him the thumbs-up sign. He gave us one back and ruffled my hair as he sat down on the railing— and startled us all when he suddenly flipped backward into the water with a huge splash.

I slowly released the air hose as Gramps dog-paddled away from the boat. I was focusing on making sure there weren't any kinks when the boat engines suddenly roared to life behind me.

Wait. What??

I jerked my head around and saw the prince at the wheel.

My blood turned to ice. What was he doing? I turned to stop him, but the ogre was right there in my face. He held up a huge paw and blew a cloud of sparkly powder in my face. Sleeping powder?? I'd seen some late-night infomercials for the stuff, but I'd never seen it in person! Wiping my face frantically, I spun around and saw that Chester and Kevin had been powdered as well.

Sleeping powder works fast, if you've never experienced it. I tried to yell "What's happening??" but it came out all garbled.

I felt my legs turn to rubber underneath me as the ogre ran to the side of the boat and cut both the anchor rope and Gramps's breathing tube. Panic came over me as I tried to fight the effects of the powder. I fell to my knees against the railing, trying to call out to Gramps.

Gramps had his helmet off and was calling back to me.

Kevin collapsed face-first onto the deck beside me, followed by Chester.

The last thing I saw before my eyes closed was

the prince's ogre inflating an emergency raft and tossing it in Gramps's direction.

The last thing I *heard* was the prince laughing and singing something that sounded like "Gonna get me some tall beans, yes I am!!"

And then I was just gone.

· 7 ·
ALL ABOUT
THE BEANS

WAKEY WAKEY, TROLL.

I came to with a start—I mean, the prince's little ferret face isn't the nicest thing to open your eyes to on a *good* day. As I looked around trying to remember where I was, a headache the size of a Lard Mammoth landed on top of my head.

RIGHT HERE'S GOOD.

Then it all came flooding back to me, as well as the realization that I was tied up. I bolted upright.

"GRAMPS!! Where's my gramps?!?"

"Aw. I see you're confused." The prince was right up in my face, and his cheese breath wasn't making my headache any better.

I MEAN, HOW COULD YOU NOT BE? YOU'VE BEEN SADDLED WITH A TEENY LITTLE TROLL BRAIN!

"Let's wake your fellow peons up and I'll explain."

With that, Trunk stepped away from driving the boat and threw a bucket of seawater onto the three of us. Chester and Kevin came awake gasping and sputtering.

TSUNAMI! BATTEN THE HATCHES!!

The prince sat on a box right in front of us and waited patiently for the other two to remember where they were. I spent the time telling him I'd kill him if my gramps didn't make it back and trying to burn his face off with my eyes.

Roquefort finally spoke up. "Everybody awake? Excellent! Because it's time I explain the real purpose of our little excursion."

Chester struck out with his foot, but the prince ducked back. The toe of Chester's goofy jester shoe missed Roquefort's chin by an elf hair.

"Ahh! Ha-ha. Not a good move, clown. One more move like that and Trunk will gladly toss you and your ridiculous hat overboard."

I felt heat coming off of Chester as he spoke.

EAT FROG WATER, YOU LITTLE $%#*@!!

Only he didn't say a series of symbols. He said the real words. I saw a tiny look of shock cross the prince's face before he went on.

"I bet you dolts thought we were way out at sea before! While you were all getting your beauty rest, we've been making excellent time."

I craned my neck to look over the boat's railing and what I saw alarmed me. For starters, there was no land to be seen. But even worse, the sky had grown a lot darker. As I looked, a bolt of lightning streaked across the sky. Kevin made a startled sound.

"I know, I know. We're headed into the storm. I hadn't foreseen that, but we're almost to the Berundi Rectangle, so we shouldn't be here long."

And that . . . is when Kevin lost his mind.

He started yelling and whining and passing out, repeatedly. Like one of those sleeping goats I've seen online.

"The Berundi Recta . . .??" Unconscious. "Have you lost your horrible little . . . ??" Out cold. "Nobody comes out of the . . . !!" Gone again.

"Shut your pig up!" Anger flashed across Roquefort's face. "So annoying!" He took a second to compose himself before going on.

"Here's the deal. You know the old story about that dairy farmer Jack? And his beanstalk? And about the magic beans he used to grow said beanstalk?"

I glared at him, listening to Kevin hyperventilating behind me.

"Anyhoo, it was a long, long time ago, and my dad's dad—Good King Fredwin—had all the magic beans in the kingdom gathered up and destroyed. I guess Sky Giants kept climbing down the beanstalks people were growing and stomping around with all their 'Fee Fi Fo Fum' nonsense. Ate some livestock and knocked over a bunch of houses."

"So he had the stalks torn down and ruled that the beans be tossed into the ocean. Into the dreaded Berundi Rectangle, to be exact."

The prince chuckled. "Let me make this simple enough that even you'll understand." He stood up to drive the point home. "Those beans had magic in them. Making gigantic beanstalks wasn't their only trick."

He stood up and looked out past the front of the boat. Then he shouted up to Trunk. "That buoy says this is it! Cut the engines!"

The engines shut off. Roquefort turned and leaned against the railing. "Now that we're on the same page, we're going to untie you . . . but with a serious warning."

Suddenly the only sound was the gentle waves lapping against the side of the boat and a low rumble of thunder. Kevin shivered.

Roquefort was really enjoying this. It was his chance to act like a supervillain in a superhero movie.

"So, I found in an old scroll—and your stupid wizard friend Rebb confirmed it—those old magic beans have crazy magic in them. The kind of magic that would make me something I've never been . . . Something I've always wanted to be . . ."

The prince looked irritated.

"No, buffoon. It would make me . . ."

We all sat there for a second, letting that sink in.

"You did all of this for a TALL PILL?!?" I felt

the troll blood surge into the tips of my ears. "You stranded my gramps in a raft at sea for something you could have done with some PLATFORM SHOES??!?"

Trunk, busy loosening my ropes, popped me on the head hard enough that my teeth clacked and I saw stars.

I stood up and stepped out of the ropes as Trunk cornered Kevin and Chester. "Try sumthin'. I dare ya."

"Listen, troll." Prince Roquefort stepped forward as the sun disappeared behind the storm clouds. "These beans don't make you just an inch taller. Or a couple of inches taller. We're talking REAL height. *NBA height.* And height is power. Just ask Trunk there."

Trunk was too busy towering over my friends

to reply. Kevin was quiet for once, lost in thought.
Then he looked up, sheepish but interested. "NBA
height? Seriously?"

The prince ignored him and kicked a box over to
me. "Time for us to suit up."

"You don't think I'm going down there alone, do
you?" The prince rolled his eyes. "And Trunk has
to stay here with these losers. There's a diving suit
in there that should fit you."

I felt that familiar kick of troll anger. It was coming up from my toenails this time. "If you think I'm
going to help you find your stupid little . . ."

The prince smiled. "That's fine, Zarf, but the
sooner we get the beans, the sooner we can go get
your gramps. I mean, we threw him a couple bottles
of water and a raft, but . . ."

I'd hate to think what could happen to a troll of his advanced age out by himself on the...

I was shaking as I ripped the top off of the cardboard box, revealing a neatly folded diving suit and helmet. "Let's get your stupid beans and get out of here!"

· 8 ·

SOGGY BEANS

I stepped up to the railing as a huge clap of thunder shook the boat, bringing a long, high-pitched squeal out of Kevin.

I turned to the prince and yelled to be heard over the gusts of wind. "This is insane. You know that, right? We'll probably get electrocuted."

"Then we'd better be fast . . ." He looked over at Kevin. "Unless you like fried bacon." He stepped up and shoved me, just hard enough that my thighs hit the railing and I flopped over backward into the water.

As soon as I went under, I was struck by the quiet. With the wind and the rumbling thunder taken away, all I could hear was my breathing and my heart pounding.

There was a splash, and as the bubbles cleared, I saw the prince next to me. He lit up two flashlights, stuck one in my hand, and indicated I should lead the way. So I swam off, making sure to give him a couple of "accidental" kicks to the faceplate.

Side note: If you have some creepy, suspenseful music handy, now would be a good time to put it on.

The diving suits are fairly heavy, so as soon as we let some air out of them, we started sinking into the darker water below. I had no idea how deep the ocean was here, but I was willing to bet we weren't going to reach the bottom any time soon.

It got darker as we sank, and my breathing started to speed up. I saw a couple of bizarre-looking fish slide past—one looked a little like Principal Haggard.

There was a blast of static, and I heard Prince Roquefort's voice in my ears.

"Try not to speak until spoken to, troll, but I had two-way speakers put in the helmets."

We passed a coral reef with the front half of a wrecked ship collapsed on top—a barnacle-covered carving of a mermaid gracing the bow.

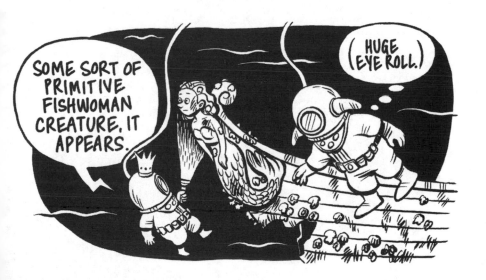

We drifted along for quite a while before we saw the first bean leaf. It was so large, I thought it was the back of a whale at first. But as soon as the whole shape revealed itself, the prince went nuts.

If we'd been on dry ground, I'm sure he would have been jumping up and down, but as we were suspended underwater, it just looked like an awkward little squirm.

THE STALKS ARE HERE!! THAT LITTLE WIZARD NERD FREAK WAS RIGHT!!!

I was stunned. I hadn't expected to find a single trace of the beans, much less these monstrous stalks.

We landed on a leaf. It was as big as a king-sized bed and barely moved under our weight. We walked to where it joined the enormous gnarled stalk, which disappeared into the dark water above and below us. It must have been six feet wide at this point.

Beyond the stalk I could just barely make out a couple of others. It was an entire grove of the things!

I turned to the prince. "We're here. Can we grab some of your beans and go?"

The prince got down on his hands and knees, peeking over the side of the leaf.

He was looking up and down the plants. "Where on the stalks do the magic beans grow?"

Groan. He couldn't have looked this up before?

I walked over and stepped off the leaf, looking for the next one to drift to. "Well, let's figure it out quick, genius." The prince got back to his feet and jumped after me. We drifted past a few leaves, inspecting the stem and all the gross squiggly strands coming off of it. I craned my neck, looking at the bottoms of the leaves and wishing I'd paid better attention in Mr. Greenthomb's botany class.

I was about to lose hope when the prince started squealing in my ear. Let's go ahead and rank that as one of the "Ten Most Annoying Sounds on the Planet."

"Eeeeeeee!! Look!! Down there!! On that other stalk!!"

I followed his flashlight beam and saw what looked like a cluster of multicolored beans, nestled in beside a thorn longer than my leg. They seemed to be lightly glowing, and about the size of those small Nerf footballs.

I was relieved to see them. We could grab a couple and head up top and try to beat the storm out of here. "Well, let's go get 'em."

We stepped to the side of the leaf and launched ourselves off in that direction.

We were falling because of the weight of the suits, on course to reach the beans . . . when I got the snot knocked out of me by what felt like a freakin' freight train.

· 9 ·

NOT SO
FAST

I think my brains got scrambled in the hit, because it took me a full minute to figure out what was happening.

I yelled at Roquefort. "WHAT WAS THAT??"

His voice was breaking up. The two-way speakers were shorting out. "It looked like . . . big green . . . extra-long school bus . . . fins!! And teeth!!"

I backpedaled to stop the spinning. I was twisting around trying to see better—which was really hard to do in this helmet—and listening to the prince have a static-filled panic attack.

IT'S... SEA WITCH!! I KNOW IT IS! IT'S FLIPPIN' URSULA!! I SAW... ITTLE MERMAID TWICE!!

Roquefort had settled on a leaf about six feet below me. Suddenly, a shape started to emerge from the dark below him. My heart jammed into my throat—it was some kind of sea serpent. A big fat one the size of a dump truck, and it was coming straight up at us.

"BRACE YOURELF!" I yelled, hoping he could hear me. "GRAB THAT LEAF LIKE YOUR LIFE DEPENDS ON IT . . . BECAUSE IT DOES!"

I thought the serpent was going to ram the prince, until it opened its cavern of a mouth. Roquefort was dwarfed by the toothy opening behind him and I couldn't look away.

The big fish-monster smashed into the leaf in an explosion of bubbles and bits of beanstalk. Its rows of sharp teeth broke through the leaf like one-ply toilet paper—and I watched with horror as Roquefort disappeared down the giant beast's throat.

I held on tight as the creature swept past. Scales the size of Frisbees rushed by, inches from my faceplate—and then it was moving away. It disappeared behind a couple of stalks and I was left in silence.

I tried to swallow, but my throat had gone dry. Had that really just happened? The prince was dead??

I couldn't stand the little jerk, but I hadn't wanted him to DIE!! I tried to calm my breathing and think.

Was that thing coming back for me?

I was untangling my air hose and fighting back a wave of fear when my speaker crackled.

". . . find out where in the name of the king I am, I'm going to THROTTLE you, you floppy-eared half-wit."

ROQUEFORT?? YOU'RE ALIVE?

He was coming in and out, but I got the important parts.

". . . of COURSE I'm . . . you fur-headed . . . seem to have fallen . . . some sort of crevasse. I can't see a thing . . . VERY tight space . . ."

He had no idea.

I explained as delicately as I could that he'd been . . . eaten. Swallowed, at the very least. Was currently being digested.

"GET ME OUT OF THIS FISH, TROLL!!! I ORDER YOU!! BY ROYAL DECREE!!"

As I hung there on the stalk, I kept imagining I saw the serpent out of the corner of my eye. That familiar panic from my nightmares was trying to overwhelm me. "Okay. Okay, okay. Let me come up with a plan."

Roquefort's voice came through quietly but clearly. "Oh, great. I'm dead."

I drifted down to a leaf by a clump of beans. I reached up and plucked a bright orange one and held it up to my faceplate like I was eating.

I had a hunch this serpent thing was guarding the beans. (It was a safe bet. There's always a dragon or mountain orc or something guarding stuff.)

At least the prince fell for my acting. "You'd better not be eating my legumes, Belford!! You're tall enough as it is!!"

And then I saw it—an approaching shape, gliding through the forest of beanstalks, the prince's air hose rising from its mouth. I had to act fast.

I reached up and grabbed on to the thorn next to the beans, taking care not to impale myself. I grabbed on with both hands and yanked. It didn't budge. I got a better grip, put my feet up on the stalk, and started pulling as hard as I could.

I looked over and the serpent was almost on top of me. I saw teeth and gums and tongue—and something inside me kicked in. Troll strength? Panic juice?

The huge thorn tore free and I clutched it to my chest just as the serpent's mouth closed down around me. I slammed into the tongue, which promptly started forcing me down the throat. I got a disgusting front-row view of gigantic tonsils as I slid past, the opening getting tighter and tighter.

GOING DOWN! NEXT FLOOR: STOMACH BILE... PARTIALLY DIGESTED ROYALTY.

I yelled out to the prince. "Okay! I'm in the serpent too. Coming your way."

There was a pause before the prince replied. "Wait . . . *THAT* WAS YOUR PLAN??? Get eaten too? BRILLIANT WORK, EINSTEIN!! Now we're BOTH dead!"

I was too distracted by my cramped, bumpy trip

down the esophagus to pay much attention. Now I knew what a wad of chewed-up food feels like.

The breath was being squeezed out of me, and I was worried I might black out—when I was dumped into a slightly larger, squishier area.

I flipped on my flashlight. There were huge bits of fish and beanstalk leaves floating around in the liquid—this had to be the stomach—and then I spotted the prince's feet. Roquefort was rolled up in a huge piece of leaf like a little prince-urrito, which explained why he couldn't see or move.

I unrolled him as quickly as I could, ignoring his complaints.

Unwrapped, Roquefort started chewing me out for being a moron—until I held up the enormous thorn I'd smuggled in.

Time for a disclaimer: I cannot claim that no sea serpents were injured in our escape. I'm sure there are some of you out there who looove man-eating demon-fish. Maybe you belong to some group that protects bloodthirsty, ocean-dwelling monsters.

All I can tell you is that I did what I had to do. I took that thorn and jammed it into the creature's stomach like I was drilling for oil. Then we, along with the rest of the contents of the stomach, lurched forward violently as the serpent came to a screeching halt.

Together we dislodged the thorn so I could cram it into the side of the stomach. There was a muscular convulsion around us, along with a stomach grumbling that threatened to burst my eardrums.

I stuck the thorn in once more—and that did the trick.

Now, I could sugarcoat the truth and tell you the creature sneezed and blew us out in a big puff of air—like in cartoons. But let's be honest. Our serpent blew chunks—us being some of the bigger chunks.

Everything in the stomach started frothing and

churning around violently, and then came the yarfing.

There was nothing comical or easy about it. It was violent and scary and disgusting, and we were shot backward up the throat like we were on the world's worst waterslide.

We shot out of the nose, snapping both of our air hoses.

I looked back and saw the serpent, its face scrunched up in pain and a nasty slice on its nostril where the thorn must have shot out. Just before it took off, it looked over and saw us. Surprise and anger registered in those big eyes.

Then it was gone—probably in search of some first aid and a bottle of Pepto-Bismol.

Water began pouring into our suits, and I started fighting to get out of mine. I took a huge breath and popped off my helmet. I kicked the suit off and headed toward the surface for some air.

When I got high enough to see the surface, the waves looked rough and sparkly like rain was hitting the water.

The storm had hit.

· 10 ·
MAKIN'
WAVES

I broke onto the surface and into a nightmare. Huge waves were everywhere, and the rain was coming down in torrents. As soon as I was swept up one side of a wave, I got smashed down the other, catching blasts of salt water up my nose. I twisted around, looking for the boat, pushing my soaked hair and ears out of my face.

I was launched up a steep hill of water, and at the wave's crest I was able to see the boat.

It's weird how time slows down in crazy moments like this. It's like your brain is going so crazy fast, everything around it seems to be standing still.

I saw the boat drifting away and getting pounded by the waves. I heard the engine trying to start. Chester was at the back, working frantically on one of the motors, and I heard him yelling to Trunk. "Try it again! Again!!"

Then I went flying down the other side of the wave. I had a split second to wonder where the prince was before I was hurtling to the top of the next wave. The boat was already another ten or fifteen feet away. Kevin was at the back railing with binoculars. (How he wasn't passed out in the fetal position will remain a mystery for the ages.) Then he spotted me and yelled as loud as he could.

I was smashed back down and shot back up, and what I saw this time took my breath away. Kevin had one round lifesaver around his waist and another in his hand, and he was diving from the side of the boat in my direction.

I forgot about the prince, the waves, the lightning . . . everything except getting to Kevin. I put my head down and swam like I'd never swam. Swum? Swummed? Whatever.

The waves were at least ten feet high at this point, so it was a bit like body-surfing on a roller coaster.

I was swimming so hard with my eyes closed that I didn't see Kevin until I crested a wave and slammed headfirst into him. I slipped into the extra lifesaver and saw a combo of crazy fear and relief on his face.

We had to yell to be heard over the storm. Kevin was full-on freaking out, and I couldn't blame him one bit. "The boat! Engines are flooded! Chester's trying to fix 'em!"

I nodded and noticed on the next wave that I could barely make out the shape of the boat through the rain.

Kevin sputtered, burped, and coughed up about a gallon of water.

I looked around the best I could, then shook my head. "Don't know."

We both scanned the area until the rain started coming down even harder. I could barely see Kev's snout a few inches away from my face. We both put our heads down and held on tight.

* * *

I'm not sure how long the storm lasted, but it felt like days. When the rain and waves slowed and finally let up, there was no sign of the boat or the prince. We were completely alone. No land in sight. Just water, water, and more water. I floated there, worrying myself sick about Chester and Gramps. I kept picturing Gramps yelling back at the boat "What's going on?" and tried not to start crying.

A while later, the sun came out and started drying us. Kevin spoke for the first time in hours.

I let that sink in for a bit. "Any elf in particular?"

Kevin thought about it. "Not one we know. Maybe a Keebler elf."

I let out a small laugh without raising my head.

A few hours went by before we spoke again. We just drifted, feeling the sun slowly turn us into beef jerky. Once, I thought I heard a boat engine, but it turned out to be some kind of bug.

When I spoke, I sounded like a desert goat with a mouth full of sand. "Have you looked around lately?"

Kevin's voice was a croak. "I opened my eyes about two hours ago. Wasn't anything to see. Just water. And I think I'm too tired to lift my lids now anyway."

"I hear that." The thought crossed my mind that we were floating shark bait, but I wasn't about to mention that to Kevin.

I must have drifted off to sleep at some point, because I dreamt I was lying in my bed and a huge Muck Beast was licking my toes.

SLURP. SLURP. SHLUUURP.

I could feel the tongue moving slowly. Slurrp. Shhlurp. Shhh. Shhhhh.

Then I was awake. I could still feel something dragging against my toes, but the sound had changed. I bolted upright.

"KEVIN!!"

We were a few feet off of a beach, my toes dragging on the bottom and waves shushing quietly onto the shore. As Kevin woke up, I stared at several huge palm trees against the blue sky. Kevin turned around and screamed. "LAND!! WE'RE NOT DEAD!!!" Then his eyes grew wide as I pulled us in.

"Wait, we're not dead, are we?? How would we know??"

WE'RE DEAD!! I KNEW IT!!

I walked up onto the sand, fell to my knees, and face-planted.

Kevin crawled up beside me and collapsed on his back. "Yeah, well . . . the day isn't over yet."

·11·

LANDED
AND STRANDED

After a while, we both sat up and took a look around. The beach curved out of sight in both directions, and I couldn't see much past the line of trees at the top of the beach.

WHERE DO YOU THINK WE ARE?

I stood up and started knocking the sand off of my shorts. "I'm not sure, but look at this place. There's probably a five-star resort on the other side. We'll be in hammocks sipping Shirley Temples before you know it."

That got Kevin on his hooves, though he grumbled as he brushed himself off.

...need fresh water more than Shirley whatevers...

...dehydration... leading cause of...

We started walking along the beach, looking for signs of life. We'd only walked five minutes before I got the sense that this island was tiny—and maybe ten minutes after that we were back at the spot where we'd left the lifesavers. Dang.

Kevin was starting to get twitchy (he does this sometimes), so I suggested we go up into the trees to see if there was a natural spring or something. The wooded center of the island looked pretty dense, with palm trees, flumpfruit bushes, and snarly vines—so who knew what we'd find.

We were almost to the tree line when a clump of bushes started shaking in front of us. Whatever was in there was a lot bigger than a muck rabbit or a squirrel. (Unless you count Mustachioed Mongo Squirrels, but they're mostly found in the northern kingdoms.)

Kevin yelped and stumbled back a few steps.

The fronds rustled a bit before they parted and Prince Roquefort jumped out.

"You're trespassing on Roquefort Island! Drop your weapons!"

I groaned and relaxed my shoulders. "We don't have any weapons, you idiot. Unless you count bad breath."

Roquefort eyed us both suspiciously. "One can never be too careful on Roquefort Island. It's a savage, dog-eat-dog place. Be warned."

He straightened and held the tip of the spear up to my nose to drive his point home.

I pushed it aside. "What happened to your clothes? And how long have you been here?"

The prince squinted up at the sky and seemed to count on his fingers for a few moments. "Judging by the travels of the sun . . . I'd say twenty minutes, at least."

I rolled my eyes and went back to help Kevin up as Roquefort went on.

"My clothes are drying on a rock back there. But how did I arrive on Roquefort Island, you might ask?"

I'M NEVER CALLING IT ROQUEFORT ISLAND. BUT GO ON.

He did. "After you COMPLETELY ABANDONED me back there, I thought I was a goner. I fought valiantly for hours, but eventually I breathed in too much water and I blacked out." He let that hang in the air for a bit.

"I woke up leaning against a palm tree over there."

I stared at him blankly. "That makes no sense. Why didn't you drown? How'd you end up in the tree line?"

Suddenly the prince turned away, mumbling and looking sheepish.

He was acting weird, so I pressed him. "I missed that. What?"

He turned around and blurted it.

"Or, like, she was part pig and part fish! I was in and out, so maybe I dreamt her, but I think she was . . ." He trailed off, probably because of the looks on our faces. "I swear if you tell anyone about this, I'll take this spear and make troll and pork shishkabobs out of—"

"Seriously?? I thought they were just bedtime stories my dad would tell me!!" Kevin was so excited, you'd have thought he'd won the mutton lottery. "Was she insanely beautiful beyond your wildest dreams?"

I'd heard of a mermaid before, but a mer-pig was new to me. Kevin was licking his hooves and using them to smooth his stray hairs and eyebrows into place.

"Maybe she'll come back! I need to freshen up— get some of the wrinkles and sand out of this shirt."

I had to smile, as both Meredith and imminent death seemed to have slipped his mind for once.

We spent the afternoon searching the island. (If I ever screw up and call it Roquefort Island, you have my permission to give me a long, deep, luxurious swirly. Seriously.)

By incredible luck, there turned out to be a small natural spring up in the trees. It was barely a trickle of water bubbling up out of the ground, but we made it work. We sipped at it until our stomachs sloshed and then sat in the shade sharing the one banana we'd found that wasn't rotten. Then we all lay back and complained for a while. (Sometimes it helps, okay?)

HOW CAN TWO BITES OF A BANANA MAKE ME HUNGRIER?

TRAPPED WITH A PIG AND A TROLL! UNBELIEVABLE!

Kevin and I managed to throw together a little shelter made of palm fronds while the prince sat in the shade fanning himself and calling out orders.

MAKE MY BED OF LEAVES EXTRA SOFT! I HAVE DELICATE SENSIBILITIES!

I somehow got through the late afternoon without strangling Roquefort. Kev and I started building a fire as the sky turned orange. Kevin was holding a piece of wood as I rubbed another against it—trying to create a spark.

"You think Chester's okay?" Kevin didn't look up from the piece of wood.

I took a break and looked out at the water.

I DO. I REALLY DO.

"Unless he cracked the wrong joke and Trunk ate him."

Kevin laughed nervously and I went on. "I mean, he's still on the boat, as far as we know. I keep thinking we'll hear him coming any time now. Or maybe he's gone back for my gramps and now the whole kingdom is out looking for us."

Kevin smiled as bravely as he could. "Well, I'm sure they have the entire navy searching for His Royal Jerkypants."

I started pushing the wood back and forth as fast as I could. "True that."

The fire finally started. (Score another for troll strength.) When darkness fell, we all sat around, trying not to think about food as we stared into the fire.

When the awkwardness in the air had built to a nice unbearable thickness, the prince excused himself to the shelter to sleep. And not two minutes later, horrible rattling snoring came echoing out of the little lean-to.

I'm not kidding. It made Gramps's snoring sound like a cute little kitten purr. Like, I think something may be seriously wrong with Roquefort's nose or face. That or he swallowed a Chainsaw Dragon.

ONE OF THE MORE ANNOYING DRAGON BREEDS

Eventually, Kevin and I gave up on sleeping in

the shelter and settled down to sleep on opposite sides of the fire. Just before I nodded off, I looked over and saw Kev staring up at the stars with big worried eyes.

·12·

ANOTHER DAY IN PARADISE

I woke up to the sound of singing, and thought for a moment that I was still dreaming. It was a girl's voice. The sound of someone singing absentmindedly to themselves. I lay there for a few seconds until I recognized the tune. "Lost at Sea" by The Sandy-Toed Minstrels. How annoyingly appropriate.

I rolled over and saw Kevin looking back with a hoof to his lips in a shushing gesture. He was pointing toward the water.

I sat up to look, and there in the waves, her snout sparkling in the early morning light . . . was a mer-pig. She was gently splashing up water to wash her long fish-tail off. Her blond hair was practically glowing as it swept back and forth across her shoulders.

I turned back to Kevin and saw that he was already full-tilt over the moon. The look of love on his face was something to behold. I was trying to get his attention when I heard the prince's voice whispering in my ear.

I couldn't help it. My head snapped around and I yelled.

The prince fell back, startled. I remembered we were trying to be quiet and continued in a whisper-yell. "WHAT IS WRONG WITH YOU??"

But it was too late. The singing stopped and I heard the mer-pig's voice.

"Wow! Y'all are finally up?"

Kevin started stammering. "I . . . well . . . how . . . you . . ."

Seeing how much trouble he was having forming words, I got to my feet and walked down the beach toward her—feeling a little woozy from the lack of food.

"Hi. I'm Zarf." I pointed over my shoulder and introduced Kevin and Roquefort. "What's your name?"

She smiled and extended her hoof. "S'wella." The way she was holding her hoof made me think she wanted me to kiss it, like in old movies, but I just gave her a fist bump to be safe.

"So . . . S'wella. You're a mer-pig?"

She threw back her head and laughed. "I guess I am—but I haven't heard that one in a while. We go by a lot of names."

SWINE MAIDS... BACON TAILS... A SERIES OF CLICKS AND DOLPHIN SQUEAKS...

"But mer-pig'll work just fine." I wouldn't have expected an ocean resident to have her light Southern belle accent.

Roquefort stepped up. "So, you're the, um . . . *thing* that saved me?"

She splashed some water over her shoulders. "I

am indeed. I saw you were in trouble, and protection's one of my sacred duties as a clickity-click tic squEEAAK clicka-ticka WHEEEE."

We must have stared back blankly, because she went on. "Sorry. Mer-pig. Force of habit."

Then Kevin stepped up beside us—slowly, like he was approaching the Queen of Everland.

HERE'S A...I PICKED YOU AN ISLAND FLOWER.

S'wella put her hoof to her chest, completely caught off guard. Then a small blush showed up on her cheeks. "Thank you . . . Kevin. Nobody's ever given me a flower before." She gave him a big smile. "But that's actually the bloom from a Poison Fantasia Bush. I'd wash your hooves right quick if you don't want itchy blistering lesions."

Kevin let out a squawk and flung the flower away before rushing into the water, scrubbing frantically at his hooves.

The prince let out an obnoxious sigh. "Can we skip the budding fish/pig romance and get to the part where you rescue us—or at least catch us some fish?"

I didn't like the way he was looking at me, so I moved a couple steps away. S'wella gave Roquefort an annoyed look.

The prince let his head fall back. "Seriously?! Seaweed?!? That's all you're gonna do for us??"

She smiled patiently. "Oh, trust me. There are plants you know nothing about. Ever had Troggle Pods?"

The prince shook his head, looking sullenly away.

"They taste just like gooey cinnamon buns. I'm not kidding. Or how about Fetzzle Stalks? They taste like mutton."

Kevin stopped scrubbing at himself and looked over.

OH, WE'RE GONNA NEED A LOT OF THOSE.

S'wella flipped her hair off her shoulders and laughed. "Oh, I'll bring you extra, Kevin. It's a ways away, so it may take me a while. Don't y'all go anywhere!"

She turned around, dove into a small wave, and with a couple kicks of her long tail, she was gone— leaving barely a ripple.

* * *

Kevin had it bad.

Roquefort snorted as we made our way back up the beach. "She's half sushi, if you didn't notice."

Kevin was horrified. "You take that back! She saved your stupid life!"

The prince chuckled as he leaned against a tree. "Look. To each his own."

Kevin's face turned red and he huffed a few times before stomping off, kicking sand everywhere.

I leaned against another tree and stared at the prince for a while. For once I wasn't so much mad as I was . . . fascinated.

Roquefort looked away like he hadn't heard me. So I went on. "No, seriously! It's in your bones. You have to be a jerk the way sharks have to swim. If they stop, they die."

"Look, troll." The prince looked over at me like he was speaking to a toddler. "You may think it's easy being the prince, but it isn't. Things are expected of me that you wouldn't even understand."

I was digging around in my ear for any remaining sand.

"Well, there are the twice-a-day wardrobe changes and my nightly moisturizing ritual and . . . and . . . NEVER MIND!" The prince started walking away.

"No, I really want to know!" I followed him. "If we have to share this stupid island, I'd like to—"

Roquefort spun around to face me.

"It's *my* island and you two are just barnacles clinging to my hull. If I had the proper . . . the proper . . ."

He was frantically making a hand gesture, so I guessed, "Scraping tool?"

"Yes. Thank you. If I had the proper *scraping tool,*

I'd scrape you right off!" He stormed away in the opposite direction from Kevin. "Leave me be, troll!"

Kevin and I spent the next couple of hours looking for food—and not finding any. I kept looking out at the water hoping I'd see S'wella returning.

Kevin was starting to freak out.

"I'm so hungry, Zarf. They're gonna find me here, all shriveled up!"

He wasn't alone in the hunger thing. Turns out it's tough to get through a boat smuggling, a fight with a sea monster, a day adrift at sea, and being stranded on an island on a measly third of a banana. I'd never been this hungry. It wasn't just my stomach anymore. My ears were hungry. My toes were hungry. Each of my teeth felt like a tiny little empty stomach.

We were still walking along hoping we'd find something to eat when we came up behind the prince sitting on a rock. His head was down, so I thought he might be asleep . . . until he turned around.

He was eating! I mean, really mowing down on something!

I've described before how sometimes my troll anger comes rushing up from my toes. Well, this time it just exploded into me—one second it wasn't there and the next moment it was. I think it was the rage and hunger combined. I took two steps and drilled into the side of the prince, both of us crashing into the sand.

"YOU'RE HOLDING OUT?? What are you eating?"

I tried to peel open the prince's hands until Roquefort shouted, his face muffled by the sand.

"Okay! Okay! It's the beans!! My magic beans!"

I was furious. "SHARE THEM, you sniveling little . . ."

But Kevin grabbed my arm. "NO! Let him have it, Zarf! We don't have any idea what those beans do!"

I'll admit—hunger may have been clouding my judgment. "Yeah, I do! They're gonna FILL MY BELLY! That's all I need to know!" Roquefort slapped my paw away, but I reached back in and got a big chunk of mushy beans away from him. I scuttled away like a wild animal guarding its dinner.

Kevin was beside himself. "Zarf, stop. You know I'm right. Those things have been in the water for decades! I'm hungry too, and nobody wants to be tall more than me, but let's see what happens to Roquefort first!"

Roquefort jumped up and backed away, cupping his little stash of beans to his chest. He started laughing like he was losing it.

"I'm going to take my rightful place as the tallest boy in Cotswin Middle School!" He turned and scampered away across the sand. "People will give me nicknames like Stretch and/or Beanpole!"

I looked around at Kevin and met his pleading eyes, but I couldn't help myself. Blame it on my troll brain. I crammed those beans in my mouth, chewed twice and swallowed.

Kevin lost it.

"S'wella's gonna bring food at any time! Those beans could be poisonous for all we know. Or the magic could have gone bad. They could turn you both into—"

I cut him off. "Stop being a worrywart for once, Kev! Just stop! Those beans are fine! Nothing is going to happen to Roquefort! You and I both know I'm—"

I stopped as a bloodcurdling scream from our bean-eating prince drifted up from the beach.

AAUUUIIGH!

·13·
BAD
MAGIC

Have you ever seen a werewolf movie? In most of the good ones, there comes a point where you get to see the main character turn into a wolf in a slow, disgusting, painful-looking way. They collapse and writhe in pain while thick hair grows out of them and their shoe size grows from a ten to a forty-three in a matter of seconds. Their nose and mouth stretch out of their face like they're . . . Anyways, you get the idea.

This was happening to Roquefort. Sort of.

As we ran up, he was down on the sand on his hands and knees, groaning. At first I thought he was going to yarf, but then I saw his legs. They were starting to turn green from the toes up . . .

And then they started to stretch.

This sight was almost more than I could handle, but it was made waaay worse by the feeling of those beans settling into my empty stomach. I felt like I'd swallowed a time bomb.

The prince looked back and saw his elongating green legs and let out a wail. I felt something in my stomach flip over as the prince's legs started to twist and—I kid you not—sprout leaves.

Kevin mumbled something about not passing out, then passed out. I had to sit down as I watched the prince's legs get longer and longer. They were looking more and more like the beanstalks we'd seen underwater. The prince flopped over so he could see what was happening.

And then the growing stopped.

Roquefort and I sat there in shock, panting, staring at his new trunk legs. They were easily four or five times as long as his old legs.

That's when my first wave of pain hit. Only mine struck in my scalp and at the base of my ears. I doubled over next to Kevin—blissfully unconscious Kevin.

It felt like someone had hooked my ears to two Speed Griffins and they took off at full speed. I could feel my hair swirling around like there was a tornado up there.

I glanced over at Roquefort, who had forgotten his new gnarly legs and was watching my head transform with a look of horror. I curled up in a ball and concentrated on breathing for what felt like hours—but was really about twenty seconds, from what Roquefort said later. And then the pain just . . . stopped.

I sat up and looked at the prince.

The stunned prince looked down at his legs and wiggled some of the roots at the bottom like toes. "Bad magic, I guess."

I noticed a thick vine hanging by my shoulder. I gave it a gentle tug and realized it was my ear, transformed. I could still hear, but it was kind of . . . half ear half vine. I was inspecting it when a big leaf fell in front of my face. I reached up into my hair, but it felt like sticking my hand in a plant.

I guess magic beans affect trolls and humans differently.

The prince exploded. "That's nothing!! Look at my legs!! I'm half vegetable! And bathing suit season is coming up!!"

Kevin stirred and sat up. There was panic in his eyes as he looked at my leafy hair and ears and then over at the prince's legs. "What did I tell you, Zarf? What did I say??" Then he crossed his arms and looked away.

The prince glared back at him. "If I could walk, I'd come over there and shove some of these beans down your . . ." One of his stalk legs bent at the knee and he stopped. "Hold the phone. Maybe I *can* come over there . . . If I just . . ."

He bent the other leg and maneuvered himself onto his knees. Then—super wobbly at first—he stood up. Sort of.

Finally he was standing—maybe six feet tall with the new stems—looking down at Kevin and me. He put his hands on his hips and looked around.

There was a loud splash in the water behind us and we all turned. S'wella was lugging a big net full of plants behind her into the shallow water.

Kevin took off running to help her—and to get

his hooves on some of that mutton plant, no doubt. He splashed into the water, gushing. "Thank you, S'wella! Thank you thank you thank you." S'wella smiled at Kevin, glowing, as he grabbed hold of the net and helped her pull. The prince and I walked up as Kevin reached in and jammed a wad of stalks into his mouth.

S'wella was watching Kevin enjoy the plants until Roquefort piped up. "Um, HELLOOOO? Princes eat first? Was nobody taught manners?"

S'wella turned around and looked up at Roquefort, taking in his new appearance.

·14·

LOVE ON THE HALF SHELL

S'wella watched with a smile on her face as Kevin and I plopped down in the water and started stuffing our faces full of plants. The cinnamon bun pods were amazing, and she'd brought another plant that tasted a little like orange soda. Of course, once Kevin got a taste of the mutton-flavored Fetzzle Stalks, he didn't care about the others.

SO GOOD...DON'T LOOK AT ME...CAN'T STOP...DELICIOUS...

The prince, on the other hand, waded in, grabbed a big armful of plants, and stalked (get it?!) up the beach to eat and sulk by himself.

We sat there happily stuffing our faces for a while, and I noticed that S'wella couldn't take her eyes off of Kevin. Finally, with some effort, she looked over at me and raised an eyebrow.

I LOVE WHAT YOU'VE DONE WITH YOUR HAIR.

Kevin laughed so hard, a chunk of stalk shot out of his nose and he started choking. S'wella slid over and patted him on the back until he got himself under control, then she turned back to me—a serious look on her face.

"You ate some of the beans, didn't you?"

I lowered my eyes and nodded.

"I was really hoping that wasn't where y'all had been." She leaned forward and wrapped her arms around her tail. "That's the sea witch's territory. She doesn't take kindly to visitors."

Kevin sprayed chewed-up stalk. "Wait, WHAT?!?"

THE SEA WITCH IS REAL??

"Ursula? She's real. Sorry to upset you, but I'm sure she knows y'all took some beans. Her entire being is tuned in to those beans. She can track them. It's like radar. Or bean-dar."

"*HE* TOOK BEANS!" Kevin stood up, pointing at Roquefort. "HIM! NOT US!"

S'wella looked down and shook her head. "That won't matter to her. Y'all just need to be careful. Lady Ursula holds a grudge worse than a beluga whale."

SHE'LL BE LOOKING FOR YOU.

"But then again, you just took a few beans. It's not like you messed with one of her children."

CHILDREN?

S'wella reached over and grabbed a Fetzzle Stalk. "That's what people call them, but they're more like . . . guards. Big dumb serpent guards. You'd know if you saw one."

My mouth went dry as I pictured a school bus–sized serpent who was probably nursing a pretty bad stomachache right about now.

MORE PEPTO!

S'wella went on, waving the stalk around as she talked. "Now, if you mess with one of her 'kids,' she'll hunt ya to the ends of the earth." She leaned back in the water. "But thank goodness y'all don't have to worry about that."

I suddenly felt ill. "I, um . . . I think I'm gonna go up in the shade and let my . . . let the food digest. Feeling kinda tired." I faked a big yawn.

Kevin looked around nervously. I thought it was about the sea witch until he spoke. Or blurted, which is more how it came out.

S'WELLA! DO YOU WANT TO GO FOR A WALK?

She looked over at him and blushed. "Really?" Then she waggled her long tail in front of his face. "But, um . . . a walk? Is that a joke?"

"What? I . . ." All the blood left Kevin's face as he got flustered. "I mean a swim!! I didn't . . . I don't . . . !"

S'wella started laughing. "I'm just messing with you, Kevin. I'd love to. But, while I can kind of flop along on dry land, it's a whole lot easier in the water. Would you mind going for a wade instead?"

Kevin got a goofy, relieved grin on his face.

"Yeah. No. That's good." He let out the breath he'd been holding. "A wade sounds good."

They got up and headed down the beach as I walked up to find a nice spot to freak out for a while. I watched them go, but I couldn't stop thinking about jabbing that thorn into the serpent's insides.

I plopped down under a tree, trying to ignore the loud prince snores coming from inside the shelter. I drifted in and out of sleep, but I was kind of losing it.

I've mentioned the nightmares I'd been having. That afternoon, on that beautiful beach under swaying palm trees, I had the worst of them. Or I should say a bunch of the worst. As I slipped in and out of dreams of wolves and weasels and serpents, it became hard to tell when I was awake or asleep.

I lay there in the cool shade sweating like I was in a furnace, my leafy hair wilting and lying plastered against my furry cheeks.

In a word, it sucked. I had doomed us all to be hunted down by a vengeful . . . What the heck was a sea witch, anyway?

PROBABLY NOT THIS

I was relieved when Kevin and S'wella came back. I got up and joined them in the water, the sun setting behind them. They were laughing and teasing each other, and I was really glad Kevin had someone to distract him. Otherwise he'd probably be curled up under a big shell somewhere.

S'wella said she had to get home or her family would be worried—and promised us she'd bring us more food in the morning.

I figured I'd ask. "Is there anything you can do to help us get home?"

S'wella smiled. "That's tricky. We're not *really* supposed to go near the mainland if we can help it. Sea rules and all."

She flopped back in the water, ready to take off. "Your best bet is to build your fire up. Hopefully someone will see the smoke."

She flipped her tail twice and was gone.

Kevin and I worked for a couple of hours building a new, larger fire on the beach before sitting down in its glow to eat more of the plants. The only time we saw the prince was when he stumbled out on his new stalk legs and grabbed some Fetzzle Stalks. He grunted something about being "super tall now" and took them back to his little man cave.

I listened to Kevin go on and on about his new love for a while before I finally flopped back and drifted off to thankfully dreamless sleep. I guess Kevin ran out of steam sometime later.

When I woke the next morning, it was to the sound of a deep chuckle and a sharp jab. I opened my eyes and realized someone was holding the tip of a sword to my nose. My eyes followed it up to the hilt, past the filthy fingers holding it, and up at one of the roughest-looking gnome pirates I could have dreamt up.

·15·

SWASHBUCKLED

Kevin woke up when the gnome spoke, and let out a strangled yelp when he saw the motley crew staring down at us. I leaned a hair to the right and saw an enormous pirate ship anchored a ways out from the shore. It must have been five or six stories tall, with more sails than I could count, but it was the sight of the Jolly Roger flying at the top that made my stomach clench.

JOLLY ROGER

(DUMB NAME. HE DOESN'T SEEM VERY JOLLY.)

There were three pirates, each one looking worse than the next. The old one seemed to find Kevin's cowering particularly funny. He kept chuckling, revealing a mouth with only a few straggler teeth left behind.

SUMMER TEETH
(SOME'R THERE,
SOME AREN'T) →

With an amazingly fast move, the old guy and the goat grabbed Kevin and me. I growled and spit and struggled against the goat, but he yanked my arms behind me and slapped a pair of rusty handcuffs on my wrists. I looked over and locked eyes with Kevin, who was in the early stages of a Code Red Flip-Out.

Then the gnome—who seemed to be in charge—spoke up.

"Arr. Arr. Ye made fast work o' them, lads, but let's think on this a spell. The ship, she's mighty full as she is."

SHOULD WE
JEST KILL 'EM
NOW?

The old one just stared blankly back at us. I gathered that he wasn't all there, if you know what I mean. Then the goat spoke up.

"Aye. I see yer point. An' this one looks like 'e's got some sorta vegetatin' scalp malady. Don't need tha' spreadin' on board, do we. Tha' round o' bunkbugs last week was bad enough."

I STILL GOT ITCHES IN ME NETHER REGIONS.

SCRATCH SCRATCH

"It's not a scalp malady!" I blurted it out. It seemed like our only chance to not end up crab food. "It's from some stupid beans! Not contagious. I ate some dumb magic beans and they made me all . . . leafy."

The three pirates' mouths dropped open in unison. They stared back for several moments before the gnome spoke in a hushed voice.

"Magic beans? You talkin' 'bout Berundi Rectangle beanstalk beans?"

I nodded and looked over at Kevin, who started nodding violently.

WELL, SHOVEL ME TUMBLERS.

The gnome's eye twitched twice before he turned and swatted the old pirate with his hat. "Shiver me timbers! Shiver me timbers, you twit. Do I need to write it out for you again?"

The old guy looked shaken. "Aye, sorry. Shiver. Timbers."

The gnome turned back to face us. "Do yeh mean ta tell me you half-wits took summa Ursula's precious beans? Is that wha' you're sayin'? Because of all the idiotic, landlubber-brained . . ."

Roquefort chose that moment to step out of the shelter, a bit wobbly on his new trunk legs.

CAN YOU PEASANTS KINDLY KEEP YOUR NOISE DOWN TO A...

He froze when he saw the pirates. They froze for a second as well, taking in the beanstalk legs. Finally, the gnome closed his eyes and rubbed his temples. "Get him too."

The prince took off down the beach with the goat pirate right behind him.

Roquefort, running for the first time on his new stems, was no match for the shorter, quicker goat. There was a diving tackle that sent up a cloud of sand and a flurry of unprintable curses before the prince was dragged back to us, cuffed and shouting.

"HEADS WILL ROLL! DO YOU KNOW WHO I AM??"

He went on for some time about how he was
the prince and how these scoundrels would rot in the
darkest dungeon pits of Notswin. After a bit,
the pirates walked off and spoke amongst themselves.

I tried to pick up what they were saying, but it
was hard to make out over Kevin's whimpering and
the prince's grumbling. The goat and the gnome
were clearly arguing—they were waving their arms
around excitedly—while the old, dim one dug
around in his nose with his pinky finger.

Finally, they came back over. The gnome put his
fists on his hips.

"Well, this is a fine mess. Frankly . . . it's above
my pay grade."

That took a second to settle in, but Kevin got there first and let out a sickening wail. "NOOOOOO!! Redbeard the Unapproachable??"

The gnome went on. "One and the same, pig. Redbeard ain't but a couple days from here, anyways. So go get some clothes on yerselves."

After we grabbed our clothes, they tossed us roughly into the back of the small beat-up rowboat they had used to come ashore. By the time Kevin, Roquefort, and I had untangled ourselves, the ship was towering over us, blocking out the sun. I saw more pirates leaning on the rail of the ship, watching as the goat guided us up to a rope ladder hanging down the hull.

WHEN REDBEARD GETS HOLD OF YA, YE'LL WISH WE'D FINISHED YA OFF BACK ON THE SAND, YA WILL.

Then he started laughing in that HAR-HAR-HAR way pirates do in cartoons and bad Chester jokes.

I was the last one shoved up the ladder. I stepped onto the deck next to Kevin and Roquefort, where we were surrounded by a group of the dirtiest, sketchiest-looking bunch of pirates this side of Treasure Island. There were elves, orcs, a couple of rough-looking trolls, two or three goblins, and a huge bear pirate who was eyeing my hair in a way I didn't care for.

YOU GOT ANY IDEA HOW LONG IT'S BEEN SINCE I HAD A SALAD?

The gnome stepped into the circle of pirates and raised a hand. The whole disgusting crew fell silent, so I figured he must be the captain.

LISTEN UP, YA BUNCHA MOUTH-BREATHERS!

"We got three more doomed to go face-ta-face with th' piercing glare o' Redbeard h'self. Three more who will fall to whatever horr'ble fate ol' Red sees fit. Let's all give thanks we're not in their pitiful shoes."

There was a moment of silence for us. The group looked at the ground, and a few took the filthy bandanas from their heads.

I heard a couple of coughs and one stifled burp, but it got pretty quiet. Then the gnome shouted again.

"Now, someone escort these three mis'rable souls to the bilge, 'n' let's pull anchor fer Dragon Noggin Island."

I was roughly grabbed by the scruff of the neck and hoisted into the air. I craned my neck around just in time to catch the bear plucking a couple leaves from my head and popping them in his mouth. It hurt bad enough to bring tears to my eyes. He gave me a glare.

NOT A WORD, OR I EAT MORE. I NEED ROUGHAGE IN A WAY YOU CAN'T IMAGINE.

We were taken down two or three levels into the bowels of the ship. Water sloshed underfoot in the dark crate-filled hallway, leading to a small moldy door. The elf carrying Kevin used one hand to flip through a huge ring full of skeleton keys and unlock it, kicking it inward. Then the three of us were tossed in and the door slammed shut behind us.

My eyes took a second to adjust to the gloom of the candlelit room. I slowly made out the shape of two figures sitting at a low table. One was large and hulking. The other was dressed in a ridiculous drugstore pirate costume.

ZARF?!? KEVIN?!

·16·

BILGE
RATS

Chester was beside himself, and I don't think he'd care if I told you he got a little misty. Kev and I did too.

"I thought you guys were goners for sure! I didn't . . . I wasn't . . . I've been just . . ." He flopped down on a big burlap sack marked RICE. "Where have you guys been? And what happened to your hair?"

I gave him a super-quick rundown of what had happened since we'd seen him. When I got to the part about S'wella, Kevin gasped, jumped up, and ran to the door.

NO NO NO! S'WELLA! HOW'S SHE GONNA FIND US??

The prince, sulking in the corner, piped up.

SHE'S HALF FISH, YOU TWIT.

"She probably has sonar in her flippers or something."

Chester looked a little confused, so I explained. "Kev and S'wella, y'know . . . they went for a walk . . ." I gave him one of those "It's Kevin, just roll with it" looks. "Kevin is kind of . . . he has some strong feelings . . ."

Roquefort snorted.

I ignored him. "What about you and Trunk? How'd you end up here?"

Chester explained that despite his best efforts, he hadn't been able to get the engines working again. Then, during the storm, the hull of the ship clipped a coral reef and started sinking.

"It went down suuuper fast. We were treading water for ages when we spotted this ship. It was just pure luck that they saw us." He looked around the tiny room.

Kevin ran up and grabbed Chester by the front of his pirate shirt. "They're taking us to Redbeard! Did you know that? REDBEARD THE UNAP-PROACHABLE!!"

Chester's eyes lit up. "I KNOW! Can you believe it? Redbeard is the coolest of all the pirates!" Then he caught himself. "I mean . . . he's also horrible, bloodthirsty, and terrifying. Maybe evil. But still . . ."

Kevin turned away, chewing his hoof. "I heard he eats people and uses their skulls and bones as drum kits!" He looked us each in the eye. "I don't want my skull to be a bongo!!"

Chester put his arm around his shivering shoulders. "Look, K. There's no reason to lose hope yet."

A voice—I'm pretty sure it was the goat pirate—came through the door, slightly muffled. "Actually, I'd say ya got pretty good reason for losin' hope . . . I mean, if there was a time to lose hope, now would be that time. What with the people-eating and the bone drums and all."

Chester sighed and rubbed the bridge of his nose.

"Sorry." The voice came again. "Wasn't trying to eavesdrop, but . . . Y'know. Givin' my two cents."

Kevin staggered over and sat down on a crate of Smutton. Then he flopped back and stared at the ceiling while we all let our situation sink in.

Chester sat back down on the rice sacks. "They left a pack of cards in here for some reason. It helps the time pass. But keep your eye on the Jolly Green Giant over there. He cheats."

Trunk stiffened in his seat. "I do not! I don't cheat."

The ogre turned away, sulking, and we all fell into silence for a while. The only sound for the next hour was Kevin groaning that he was getting seasick again.

My mind kept going back to Gramps, and whether he was okay. He was no spring chicken, but he was a tough old guy. I'd heard a story once that he took on three Swamp Goblins that jumped him in an alley back around the time I was born.

So . . . he had that that going for him . . . but I couldn't stop thinking about him all the same.

An hour later, we heard keys rattling at the door. When it swung open, the gnome captain was there, surrounded by several of his men.

Chester looked up at him and chuckled. "Not in public."

Five minutes later, we were all on deck with mops, buckets, and hard-bristled brushes. The pirates were really enjoying watching us scrub away.

Prince Roquefort looked like he might cry as he crawled around picking at dried bits of algae and chewing tobacco.

Then he started going on about how that position was "crimping his stalks."

As miserable as we were, this got Chester and me giggling to the point where we could hardly hold our mops. Then suddenly the captain was in front of us again. "You lot seem like a coupla real go-getters, ya do. How'd you like to move up in the biz'ness?"

Chester composed himself. "Seriously? That sounds great."

Five minutes after that, Chester and I were fifty feet up the mainmast, scraping dried bird poop off of the crow's nest.

The one benefit to working in the crow's nest was that Chester and I could speak freely without anyone listening in. And when we got down on the floor of the little platform, no one below could tell if we were working at all. So naturally, we chilled out for a while.

"WHAT?!?" I almost hurt my neck twisting to gape at him.

Chester suddenly looked serious. "I'm not kidding, Z. If I joined, maybe I could get 'em to let you all go . . ."

I stared at him for a minute. "I think you breathed in too much bird poop dust. That's insane."

Chester looked away in a "Chester in Deep Thought" way. It's not a look I see from him very often. "Is it? I'm clearly no court jester. All my jokes do is annoy people. I mean, before you got here I was telling some knock-knock jokes to lighten the mood in our little cell . . ."

"It still hurts."

That hung in the air as I pictured the scuffle.

"Maybe jokes just aren't your thing." I pushed his shoulder with mine.

Chester looked annoyed. "Isn't that what I just said?"

"No. Well, yes, but let's think about this . . ." I leaned forward. "Jokes . . . I mean, *joke* jokes . . . Maybe that's your dad's thing. He's good with the funny walks and the knock-knocks and all that."

I went on. "No, listen. What if—and this is if we survive all this—you changed your whole approach?"

I MEAN, YOU'RE A FUNNY GUY. JUST NOT WHEN YOU TRY SO HARD.

Chester was giving me a blank stare.

"What if you told stories instead of jokes? Things that happened to you? That stuff is great! Like when you had to wear Coach's underpants."

SHORTS. THEY WERE SHORTS.

I went on. "Whatever. Your stories are hilarious! It's your jokey jokes that make me want to tape your mouth shut and shove you off a tall building."

Chester looked off, and it took me a second to realize he was tearing up a little. "That . . . that's the nicest thing anyone's ever said to—"

He was interrupted by a loud growl/shout from the bear pirate at the front of the ship.

We jumped to our feet and searched the water. It took a moment to spot it. It was just a speck on the horizon at that point. Someone fired a cannon, making my heart jump into my throat, and the bear yelled again.

I stared at that tiny island in the distance and my blood turned to frozen slush.

·17·

THE BIG CHEESE

As the island grew closer, it was easy to see why it was called Dragon Noggin Island. It was shaped a lot like a huge lava dragon skull, complete with smoke from a fire coming up from what resembled the nostril area. I can't imagine there's a creepier-looking island on the planet.

Chester and I were back on the deck with Kevin, who was beside himself with worry.

We were all back in our shackles, and the moments dragged on as the island slowly grew larger. I looked over and saw a single bead of sweat roll down the side of Trunk's face. Clearly he was worried too.

Roquefort looked down at the scrawny pirate next to him. "How would you describe this Redbeard's feelings about the Royal Family?"

We came around the side of the island and spotted two long, rickety docks on wobbly-looking stilts. Another slightly smaller ship was docked at one, and I saw its name as we got closer. *Ye Old Dinghy of Death.*

How charming.

There was a large wooden sign over the end of the dock. It was NOT a welcome sign.

The crew sprang into action as we pulled alongside the dock, some jumping out and catching huge coils of rope and tying the ship up. There was a lot of yelling and scurrying around as sails were lowered and secured—I've never heard the word *Arr* so much in my life.

It was pretty annoying. I don't think they even realized how much they said it. Like people who say "like" all the time.

We were prodded off of the ship at sword-point by the captain. I finally heard someone call him by his name, Captain Gerome. I was registering the fact that he was Gerome the gnome when he started lecturing us again.

ALL RIGHT, YA BUNCHA BILGE MONKEYS.

"Yer time grows near. We'll be taking ya ta Red-beard, and we'll see what's what. Invadin' Redbeard's waters. Stealin' the sea witch's beans. These ain't small offenses 'n' I'm mighty glad I ain't you right now . . . Now git walkin'."

We were led up a small path surrounded by exotic plants, and I noticed that Kevin was surprisingly quiet. His eyes had a faraway look like he might be in shock. I came up beside him and nudged him. "You okay?"

He looked up at me with worried eyes and sniffed.

DUMB QUESTION, ZARF.

Now, if you have a weak stomach, you might want to turn away for a moment. We came around a corner to see a number of skulls perched on top of long sticks.

I heard Kevin gasp—or it's possible it was me. There were more signs warning us away, and one complete skeleton leaning against a rock.

We came through a parting in the trees covered in sinister-looking vines to find a small gathering of huts built against the side of a cliff. There were holes and caves all up and down the cliff, some with rickety ladders leading to them.

It was a filthy place. There were several clotheslines draped with striped shirts, bandanas, and cloth eye patches. Several scraggly pirates sat on their crooked front stoops, carving scrimshaw. They gave us suspicious looks before going back to their whittling.

The largest hut, at the back of the clearing, seemed to be the best looked after, aside from a scattering of bones and skulls lying to the side of the front door. As we walked up, the door slammed open. Kevin yelped and ducked behind Trunk.

It was dark inside the hut, so I couldn't see anyone there at first. But I heard a voice. It came out in a low, creaky rumble that set my teeth on edge.

I felt light-headed as the voice went on. "What sorta trash do you bring before me? Captain Gerome? Explain, lest I kill ye all."

Gerome stepped forward, looking nervous.

"Trespassers, Redbeard. Found 'em in yer waters. An' they stole some o' the witch's beans."

I BROUGHT 'EM RIGHT TO YA, I DID.

The silence from the hut seemed to last forever. Finally I heard a disgusted grunt, followed by heavy footsteps. My knees grew weak as I saw the shadows part. The tip of a beard the color of burning lava slowly emerged, followed by the legend. The one and only.

Redbeard.

BRING 'EM FORWARD.

I heard someone collapse to the dirt. I turned to check on Kevin, and was surprised to see it was Trunk. Out cold.

Redbeard was a bit shorter than I'd imagined, but made up for it in sheer . . . presence. We were brought forward (Trunk was dragged) and made to kneel.

Someone smacked the prince over the head and—what do you know?—he kneeled.

Redbeard stared at us for what felt like an eternity, playing absently with that unruly beard—staring in particular at my leafy hair and Roquefort's stalk legs.

"Tell me why I shouldn't just string yeh up now."

Nobody said anything for a moment, so I started.
I told the story as quickly and sincerely as I could,
as if at any moment a timer would go off and we'd
be done for. Chester jumped in to tell his part
and add some humor. The boat. The mutiny. The
serpent. The storm. The island. The beans. We
acted some of it out for effect.

When we finished, Redbeard just stared. Roquefort piped up.

I SHOULD CLEAR UP THE FACT THAT I'M THE FIRSTBORN SON—HENCE THE PRINCE—OF MY EXALTED FATHER, THE KING OF—

Redbeard waved a dirty hand. "Silence! I couldn't give two rats about yer royal . . . ridiculousness." He turned to Kevin and leaned forward. "Pig. This troll an' the clown . . . they tellin' the truth?"

Kev started nodding like a bobblehead doll. "I swear they are. I give you my word as a . . . as a Cotswin Middle School Prancing Knight."

Redbeard jerked. It was like someone had jabbed him with a cattle prod. His eyes got wide and started darting back and forth between us. "Wait. What did you say?"

NO, NO! NOT A REAL KNIGHT!

Kevin swallowed hard and looked over at me. I started stammering, worried they thought we were military.

"That's our school mascot! The Prancing Knights. I know, it's a horrible mascot name, but they've been trying to get it changed, and . . ."

Redbeard looked at Kevin. "Just . . . hold on. Did you say Cotswin?"

He squeaked out an answer. "Yessir. Cotswin Middle School. In the Village of Cotswin."

IN THE KINGDOM OF NOTSWIN.

Roquefort started up again. "Right. Of which I am THE PRINCE and—"

Redbeard shushed Roquefort again and paced the front stoop for a moment. He was really worked up about something. He was muttering and seemed to be having some kind of argument with himself, before he walked up and stood right in front of me.

TELL ME. DO YOU KNOW A GIRL NAMED SIERRA?

· 18 ·

SECRETS
AND LIES

My troll brain sputtered, overheated, and stalled like an old car. Had I heard that right??

"D-did you say . . . umm . . .?"

Redbeard grabbed my shoulders. "Sierra Scarlet! Do you know her?"

I immediately went into protective mode. I didn't like the idea of this mangy pirate even knowing Sierra's name.

"Si—Sierra? Scarlet, you say?? Hmm. No, I don't . . . I don't think I know such a person. If she even exists."

Redbeard gently squeezed my arm. "She's not in danger, I give you my—"

Roquefort stood up. "He's stalling! He's practically dating her. Or he'd like to think so."

Redbeard looked me in the eyes and I saw something soften in his eyes. That sounds like mumbo jumbo when you read it in a book, but it's true. Something in those eyes relaxed.

Redbeard reached up and, in one quick move, pulled off his hat, wig, and scraggly red beard, revealing a woman underneath. I must have staggered backward, because I felt someone's hand steady me.

Along with the beard, the rough, scratchy voice was gone—just like that.

Now there were tears in her eyes.

I caught my breath. "Um, she's . . . she's good. Great, even. But I don't understand what's . . ."

I was stunned. And really, really confused. I looked around at Kevin and Chester, who seemed just as dazed as I felt. I spotted the leaf-eating bear, dabbing at his eyes with a handkerchief.

I turned back as Redbeard was removing her coat. But it was more than a coat. It was a thickly stuffed costume coat, which had almost tripled her size.

YOU'RE RED RIDINGHOOD?

Her eyes went wide, and I could see panic in them. "How do you know that? Do the people back home know??"

She clapped her hands and called out to the pirates.

"Okay, gang. Here's what's happening. I'm going to go for a walk with . . . um . . ." She looked over at me.

"Zarf."

"I'm going for a walk with our new friend Zarf here. We've got a few things to discuss."

As she took off the rest of her Redbeard costume, she told the pirates to "drop the act" and prepare a feast for their new guests.

"Go all out, okay? I'm talking the works."

FIRE UP THE GRILLS, DON'T SKIMP ON SODA, AND BREAK OUT THE NICE, THICK PAPER PLATES!

The pirates looked like excited kids as they sprang into action. Red led me off down a path behind her hut. I looked back to see an elf pirate smiling and offering Kevin a huge cup full of punch.

The path curved around to a beach, where we climbed a grassy hill to a rocky spot overlooking the water. We sat down with our backs to a bush full of big tropical flowers.

ALL RIGHT, MR. ZARF.

"How do you know who I am? Did Sierra tell you alone? Or is her secret out?"

"Well . . ." I wasn't sure where to start. "Yeah. Everybody knows."

The color drained from Red's (Mrs. Riding-hood's?) face. "Oh, no. No no no." She was starting to breathe hard. "When the stupid Big Bad Wolf finds out, he's gonna make a beeline—"

I cut her off. "It's okay! He's in jail. We all thought he was dead, and he wasn't . . . But we took care of him . . . and the rest of the wolves sorta scattered in the wind."

Red stared back at me for long enough that I started to get uncomfortable. "How?"

I gave her a quick version of the story. How word had gotten out. The wolves taking over Littlepig Manor. How Sierra and I, along with our friends, had stopped Big Bad. Red was delighted by the story and stopped me several times to ask for juicier details.

SHE YANKED HIS PAW FUR? OH, THAT'S MY GIRL!!

Red was looking out at the waves smiling when I felt something tugging at my leaf hair. I jumped and twisted around. One of the blooms on the bush was chewing at my hair vines.

Red reached over and swatted the flower. "Sorry. Nibble Blossoms. I should have found a better place to sit."

The flower shrank back into the bush like it was sulking. "Oh, and one of the guys back there is a wizard. He can fix . . . all that. Your hair."

Then she fell quiet again for a while. I sat there watching seagulls fly by, enjoying the wind in my leaves. When Sierra's mom spoke again, it was almost a whisper.

"So . . . I can go home. I can see my daughter." She dabbed at her eyes with her sleeve. "This whole thing, Zarf—the island, the big scary pirate goof, the Redbeard stuff—it was all to keep her safe. To keep the wolves at bay . . . throw them off the scent. I needed people to think she and I were dead."

This was making my head hurt. "But . . . I mean . . . you really *are* kind of a pirate now, aren't you?"

WHAT WITH THE SHIPS AND THE SKULLS ON SPIKES AND ALL.

Red let out a burst of laughter that sounded exactly like Sierra. "HA! Not hardly." She grabbed my arm. "Those skulls and bones are plastic. I'm surprised you couldn't see the seams. And most of those 'pirates' down there just come out here for a couple of months at a time. It's like pirate fantasy camp."

My troll brain was struggling. "But . . . what about Captain Gerome?"

She smiled. "Gerome's an accountant ten months of the year. He just likes to come out here and blow off some steam—act all fierce after tax season."

"They're a sweet bunch, really. They all know my real Ridinghood identity. I just need them to act tough, fire some cannons to scare ships from time to time . . . and go home and spread rumors about the awful horrible Redbeard the pirate so people don't come sniffing around."

I shook my head. "Redbeard the Unapproachable."

She chuckled. "Is that what they call me?"

She stood up and gave me her hand. "Here's what we'll do, Mr. Zarf. We're gonna get some food in you all, and in the morning we're gonna hightail it for Notswin." She was beaming with excitement. "I have a daughter to see."

We started down the hill to the beach, and I asked her the question that was nagging at the back of my brain. "About the, um . . . sea witch. We took some beans. Is that really as big a deal as we were told? Is she gonna . . ."

Red hopped the last few feet to the beach. "Well, it's not nothing. But don't you worry your leafy little head about it. I'll take care of the sea witch."

·19·

HAIR TODAY, GONE TOMORROW

As we made our way around the path, I heard music and chatter coming from the pirate village, followed by a huge burst of laughter. It sounded like the party was in full swing. I stepped into the village wondering what was so funny.

Chester was sitting on an old rum barrel telling a story, surrounded by the mangy-looking fake pirates. They were completely absorbed in his tale, and broke into loud laughter again as I stepped up.

The bear from earlier was wiping his eyes from laughing.

YOUR FRIEND CHESTER IS KILLING ME! I GOTTA CATCH MY BREATH!

He put his paw on my shoulder and leaned in. "Listen. I hope there's no hard feelings about earlier. We put up a prickly front until we know everything's cool. Can't be too safe when it comes to covering Red's tracks."

I assured him it was fine, and he went on to tell me he was a retired high school chemistry teacher.

YEAH... NOTHING LIKE THE SEA AIR TO BLOW THE AMMONIA SPILLS AND SPITWADS OUT OF YOUR SOUL.

When I asked about the whole eating-my-hair thing, he looked kind of embarrassed and confessed that they'd been on the boat a long time and he really *had* been craving some greens.

I found Kevin at an old picnic table going to town on a huge plate of mutton. He smiled a big greasy smile when he saw me, but kept eating.

I sat down across from him and stuffed a big juicy bite in my mouth.

"Can you imagine the look on Sierra's face?"

Kevin shook his head and laughed through a mouthful of food.

Roquefort and Trunk were sitting on the front porch of one of the homes, sullenly picking at their bowls of food and watching the festivities. The prince saw me watching him and made an obscene gesture.

Chester came panting up to the table like an over-excited puppy.

"You were so right, Zarf! I haven't told a single jokey joke and they can't get enough!" He grabbed a hunk of mutton—despite Kevin trying to swat his hand away—and made his way back into the party.

Red walked up with an old guy with a long white beard who looked like he'd been into the rum.

"Zarf, this is the wizard I was telling you about—Ferlin."

PLEASED TA MEETCHA, ZURF.

He started inspecting my leafy hair, making interested "Hmmm" sounds. Finally he got a big grin on his face and tapped the side of his head. "Aha. Yep. I know whatcha need ta get fuzzy again. Got just the thing. An' for that brat with the broccoli legs too. Don't go anywhere." He shuffled off toward one of the huts.

Red and I walked over to Roquefort and Trunk. When we stepped onto the porch, the prince sniffed and looked away, annoyed.

OH, JOY. THE TROLL AND THE DEADBEAT MOM ARE HERE.

Red took two steps and kicked the back leg of Roquefort's chair out from under him. He slammed to the floor with his big green legs flailing. Trunk jumped up, ready to do his bodyguard thing until Red put a finger to his chest, the other pointed down at the sputtering prince. I'd seen that sudden fire in the eyes before—in Sierra.

"Listen up, you little toad. I may not have been born a pirate, but I've taken to it like a natural—so you might not wanna test me. I've had enough of your snotty little royal attitude. I'm trying to help you, but right now I'd rather put you right back out to sea."

Roquefort's mouth kept opening and closing like a fish gulping air. Trunk backed up two steps and raised his paws.

Red grabbed Roquefort by the arm and helped him to his stalks.

"A friend of mine is gonna come over and fix your legs, and I suggest you treat him with respect. One word from me and he'll turn your top half into a stick of asparagus as well. Got it?"

Roquefort nodded, though you could see the anger seething behind his eyes. Red turned and gave me a quick wink and a smile. As she strolled away, she yelled back over her shoulder, "We set sail at dawn."

DON'T BE LATE, YOUR HIGHNESS!

Roquefort's face turned beet red and he started shaking. Then he let out a string of loud curses, spun around a few times, and started kicking the side of the hut with his stalks. It was really something to see.

$%*##!! !!@%$?#! $@!##$@!!

By the time Ferlin arrived with a beat-up old JanSport backpack full of small bottles and vials, the prince had pretty much worn himself out.

After digging around in his pack for a few minutes, he brightened, handed us each a bottle, and told us to gulp 'em down. I already had mine to my lips when Ferlin's eyes went wide. "WAIT, WAIT, WAIT!! SWITCH THOSE!"

I looked down at my bottle, a little freaked out, before handing it to Roquefort. He handed me his, eyeing the wizard suspiciously.

Ferlin let out a loud laugh. "Nothin' good, that's fer sure! Am I right? HA-HA-HA! I got bottles in here that'd do all kindsa awful business!"

I stared at the strange old man, alarmed, before gulping down the bitter liquid. Then I sat down and waited, my confidence in him a bit shaken. But a few moments later, my entire body started itching like it was covered with Itchy-Awful Worms.

I curled up in a ball and started scratching away at my vine ears and scalp. It felt like they were on fire until, right under my paws, I felt the leaves change. They stretched out thinner and thinner until I was scratching away at a head of normal troll hair. I felt for the vine ears, but they were gone—replaced once again with my old floppy ones.

I'd never been so happy to feel those big dumb ears in my life.

I looked up and saw the prince glaring down at his once again stubby little human legs. He didn't look happy.

· 20 ·

MORE
WATER

The party went well into the night. There was a limbo competition and a few heated matches of "Pin the Butt on the Snuffweasel." Chester and Kevin and I decided to call it a night when one of the pirates wanted to play "Spin the Peg Leg."

The next thing I knew, the bear pirate was waking us up.

"Rise and shine, mates. I was s'posed ta bring ya breakfast in bed, but I . . . I ate it."

There was a lot of moaning and sighing as we pulled on our filthy clothes, but we eventually emerged from the hut—as ready to go as we were going to be.

On the ship, we all stood off to the side with Roquefort and Trunk while the crew bustled around us. Supplies and huge coils of rope were hauled on board while they belted out pirate songs and sea chanteys.

The sun was barely over the horizon when our ship backed away from the dock. Kevin was loaded up on Dramamine and an anti-nausea potion Ferlin had given him.

I was watching Dragon Noggin Island grow smaller behind us when Red stepped up.

"Okay, gentlemen. This trip'll take a day or so if we really put the pedal down. Up for doing a couple hours of work?"

Roquefort made a disgusted noise.

Red stared at the prince. "Fine, Your Royalness. You get the choicest job of all." She pointed over at a huge pile of chamber pots. "I need you to scrub all of those out. And it's been a while, so you might need a chisel."

Roquefort swooned and looked like he might pass out. Red signaled an elf pirate, who led the stunned prince and ogre off to their duties.

Red turned to us. "Chester, this is tough, but I'm gonna need you to hang out down in the kitchen and keep the crew's spirits up. A few of your stories should do the trick."

She went on. "And Kevin? I'm so sorry, but I have several sacks of mutton jerky down there. I need you to test it for quality."

A huge smile spread across Kev's face and he started rubbing his hooves together.

I WAS BORN FOR THIS.

Red walked me over to help her steer the ship. We climbed some steps and she grabbed the big wheel. "I really just thought this would give us a chance to talk more."

I looked down at the deck to where the prince was on his hands and knees scrubbing a pot. He paused for a second and made a loud gagging noise.

RETCH!

Red laughed. "I kinda thought you'd enjoy the view too."

A gust of salty wind came along and blew through my hair. Nothing but blue skies and calm seas stretched out before us. I took a deep breath and closed my eyes, taking in the moment. When I opened them, Red had hers closed as well.

A few minutes later, Red snapped out of it—like coming out of a dream—and turned to me. "So, you're probably wondering how a mother could leave her daughter for this long, huh?"

I was caught off guard. I'd actually been thinking about nachos.

"What? No! I mean, you had your reasons."

Red stared at the boards of the deck for a while before responding. "It was bad after my run-in with the wolf. Really bad. Big Bad almost got me on a number of occasions." She absentmindedly rubbed at a faint pink scar running the length of her arm. "It was no life for a young girl, no matter how well I trained her." She cleared her throat.

I looked up and realized she had tears in her eyes. I looked away.

Red wiped a tear from her eye and let out a choked laugh. "Some big nasty pirate I turned out to be, huh? Blubbering up a storm."

I smiled and lightly patted her on the back, hoping that was the right thing to do.

Red put her arm around me and pulled me in tight. "You're a good guy, Zarf. You're all right in my book."

She let me take the wheel while we talked about Sierra. She had about a million questions, and it was a pretty easy topic for me to go on about. We were both laughing when Kevin and Chester walked up.

Chester—being a boat guy—jumped at Red's offer to steer the ship, while Kev said he was just going to go hang by the railing. I thought he was getting sick until he grabbed a pair of binoculars and started scanning the waters—more lovesick than seasick.

I came up beside him. "No sign of her?"

Kevin lowered the glasses without taking his eyes off the water. "She'll come. She has to."

I left him pining away as I went off looking for food. On my way to the hull, I passed Roquefort and Trunk, leaning against the railing rubbing huge quantities of Purell into their arms and faces.

· 21 ·

ABSOLUTELY
STUNNING

The day went by fairly quickly, and after the evening meal of Smutton and nasty canned Swamp Roots, I collapsed into an empty hammock in the bunk room.

I woke up during the night to loud snoring. I assumed it was Roquefort, having heard his talents on the island, but there was just enough moonlight coming through the portholes for me to see that it was Ferlin. He was two bunks over, using his ratty old potion backpack as a pillow and sawing away like a champion.

I drifted back to sleep feeling a sense of well-being and excitement for the future that I hadn't felt for a long time.

It didn't last long.

I was shaken awake by small hooves.

I sat up and flipped the hammock, crashing nose-first into the floor below.

I was dazed and crabby as Kevin grabbed my paw and pulled me up the stairs. For the dead of night, it was surprisingly bright on deck due to a full moon and about a bazillion stars. The wind had picked up a bit, and Kevin had to yell as he pulled me to the rail.

I looked down into the water, and there was S'wella, darting along beside the ship. She dipped in and out of the waves, shouting and gesturing like crazy. There was no mistaking the panic on her face.

Kevin and I scrambled around until we found a gigantic coil of rope and tossed it over. S'wella dodged the falling tangle before launching herself out of the water and grabbing on. Kev and I started pulling as hard as we could.

When we got her high enough, S'wella flipped herself over the rail and landed on the deck with a splat. She was so worked up, she could barely get the words out.

"Ursula . . . Gasp . . . Coming for you."

S'wella was busy gulping air, so she touched her hoof to her snout and pointed at Kevin in an "On the nose" gesture.

My blood ran cold. "Where . . . I mean . . . How soon?"

S'wella shook her head. "Any minute. I tried to get out ahead of her and her 'children' . . . but they're fast. If y'all have an alarm, sound it. Now."

Something slammed into the side of the boat—hard enough that Kevin and I were knocked off our feet. Whether it was the witch or one of her freaky serpent kids, it had to be big. I ran to the railing and couldn't believe my eyes.

The water looked like it was boiling, there were so many serpents surrounding the ship. It was an army of the creatures that had swallowed Roquefort and me. Two of them smashed into the hull as I heard the door to the lower deck slam open.

Gerome the gnome was the first one out of the door, followed closely by Red and Harry the bear.

Chester was next out the door, running into Harry's backside. He straightened his vest and stood with his hands on his hips.

Then he saw the sea serpents, and all of the blood and enthusiasm ran out of his face. "Holey buckets!"

The rest of the crew was piling out from below-decks as the ship was pummeled by the monsters. Red jumped to the top of a barrel, holding tight to the center mast as she barked out orders.

"But aim carefully! We have a limited supply!"

Chester looked over at me, confused. "What are stunpoons?" I shrugged my shoulders as Harry ran up and put a modified harpoon gun and a few harpoons in each of our hands. The pointy tips of the harpoons had been replaced with what looked like bags of sand.

"Ha." Harry put his gun to his shoulder and sighted in on a serpent. "That's 'cause you haven't seen them in action."

He pulled the trigger and the stunpoon took off like a small rocket. It left a trail of smoke, and a second later made loud contact with the side of the serpent's face. The giant fish-thing went flying, and the crew let out a huge cheer.

He started loading up another stunpoon. "He'll be alive . . . but he may wish he wasn't."

I spun around and spotted Kevin at the side of the ship. S'wella was still scootching herself across the deck, but he already had his gun up to his shoulder, aiming. I guess love makes you brave. Or at least makes you fake it.

Look . . . I'm no whiz in physics class, but I could see what was coming. I shouted his name and took off running, but it was too late. The rest happened in slow motion.

The stunpoon shot out of the gun and the force lifted Kevin off of his feet. A startled Kevin and his gun shot backward into the air like a Rocket Dragon in a hurricane. I dove to grab his hoof as he sailed overhead, but missed him. I landed and flipped over just in time to see Kevin slam back-first into the main sail. The gun punched a hole in the sail and kept on going as Kevin rolled down the canvas, getting snarled up in some ropes.

He ended up hanging about a foot over the deck, his legs tangled in the rigging.

I ran over to help him as the sound of the crew's stunpoons filled the night. So did the smacks of those sandbags drilling into serpents. As soon as Kev was free, I ran to the railing.

I put the gun to my shoulder, braced my feet, and fired at a long, bumpy serpent about twenty feet out. I'm not gonna lie. Seeing that stunpoon whomp into its slimy head felt pretty good.

I was loading up again when I caught something out of the corner of my eye. While the other serpents were swimming more or less the same direction as the ship, one was coming straight at me. I thought I recognized its shape. Then I noticed first aid tape on one of the nostrils and I knew for sure.

I fired my stunpoon as the serpent launched itself out of the water at me, but my aim was off. It glanced uselessly off the side of the beast's cheek as it sailed up and blocked the moon and stars.

My paws slipped on the wet deck as I tried to scramble backward, and I was slammed to the boards by the big elephant-sized fish.

Amazingly, my innards didn't get squeezed out

of my ears, but my nose did get jammed into my brain. I was gulping little sips of air as the thing squirmed around on top of me. I think its goal was to pancake me to death.

SHORT STACK OF ZARFCAKES WITH BUTTER AND MAPLE SYRUP

I was about to lose consciousness when I felt several muffled thuds and the serpent went limp. I was pretty sure it'd been stunpooned. A few long moments went by with my lungs screaming for air before part of the weight came up off of me. I gasped and peeled my smashed eyelids open. Holding the front end of the beast up over his head was Harry. He smiled down at me and I did my best to coax a smile out of my rearranged face.

THANKS, HARRY.

"You can eat my hair any day."

It took several of the pirate ogres and giants to help him throw the serpent overboard. I staggered up and saw that there were only a couple of serpents left attacking the ship. Chester got off one of the final stunpoons to help finish the job.

A cheer went up from the crew when the sea around the ship was calm again. Pirates of every kind slapped high fives in celebration. Even Trunk the ogre had a big grin on his face as he fist bumped a gnome back by the bow—which got me looking around. Where was Roquefort? Probably hiding in a closet somewhere.

I walked up to Kevin, who was just now starting to tremble—though he was trying to play it cool for S'wella.

"Sh-shaking? Me? Maybe just a little chilly or

something, but I'm fine. Juuuust fine. Not freaking out a bit."

S'wella smiled and gave him a peck on the cheek.

His eyelids drooped and his shaking slowed down.

I was starting to laugh when a huge can of Smutton rolled past me, gaining speed as it made its way to the front of the ship. The back of the ship was lifting.

The sea was swelling behind the ship. A giant bulge wider than our ship was rising up. It was lifting the back of the boat like a huge wave. I turned around and found Red standing beside me. "What is it? A tidal wave?"

Red's eyes were huge in the moonlight. "No."

"It's her."

· 22 ·
THE LADY
COMES CALLING

IT'S THE
SEA WITCH.

Just then the mound of water parted to reveal the top of a hair-and-seaweed-covered dome. It was enormous—maybe a school bus length across—and coming fast. I still wasn't sure what I was seeing until its eyes cleared the surface. Red glowing eyes the size of cars. That's about the time my knees went weak.

BIG... OH, WOW.
SO VERY, VERY
BIG.

Suddenly Chester was at my side with his weapon ready. "Let's see how this thing likes getting its bell rung." With that, he fired a stunpoon right into the sea witch's face. We all held our breath, wondering what would happen.

The answer was a resounding "Nothing." It bothered the sea witch about as much as if I flicked a Q-tip at your face.

That's when the rest of the head cleared the water. It was one of the ugliest things I'd ever seen. Sweeping back from the head—coming out of the thin hair—were huge writhing tentacles. There really wasn't a nose, just a couple of nostrils. And then there was that horrible mouth.

It opened to reveal hundreds of small sharp teeth. It reminded me of Ernie's mouth on *Sesame Street*—an evil, fanged, twenty-five-foot-wide Ernie mouth. I let out a nervous giggle and worried that I might be losing my mind.

A couple more stunpoons fired off with no effect, and someone was yelling that those were the last we had.

I staggered back and yelled over to Red. "That thing looks NOTHING like Ursula from *The Little Mermaid* movie!! NOTHING!!"

Red had spun a mounted cannon around at the creature. She wasn't taking her eyes off the witch while she lit the fuse. "I'd imagine they . . . didn't want to give kids . . . nightmares."

We did. But when it came, the blast was deafening. My hearing dropped out, so what happened after that was like watching a silent movie.

The cannonball hit the witch in the eye. Great, except it sent her into a rage that would have made my troll ancestors proud.

The witch reared back in a fang-bearing roar. All of a sudden there were enormous tentacles everywhere. Not like the ones on her head—these were long muscled arm suckers bursting out of the water. Two of them came up from the right side of the boat and smashed through the railing. An extra-long one shot out and slashed through the main sail. Another smashed the cannon like it was made of Silly Putty.

I turned around looking for Kevin, and what I saw was a nightmare. Kevin and S'wella were midships, avoiding tentacles like they were in the worst game of dodgeball ever.

Gerome and Harry had been swept up in two tentacles and were fighting with everything they had.

Several pirates, including Ferlin the wizard and a young female elf, were sprawled on the deck unconscious, and it suddenly hit me: This was our fault. Okay, maybe mostly Roquefort's fault, but if we hadn't dropped into their lives, these people would be safe and sound playing Pictionary on their island.

That old, unstoppable troll anger boiled up—but this time it was different than ever before. This time a good part of it was aimed at myself.

In two seconds flat, I was in a full rage. I grabbed the first tentacle I saw and snapped the end off over my knee like it was a string bean. I spun and used the end as a club to beat the rest of the tentacle back.

I'm not sure how long this lasted, but I may have gone a little bonkers—one of the hereditary hazards of being a troll. I was pounding, slashing, scratching, biting . . . I'm not sure how many tentacles I damaged, but the stupid things kept coming. I was wondering why they had named this thing a sea witch and not a Gigantic Endlessly-Squid-Tentacled Sky Scraper Ernie Puppet Mind-Melting Vision of Unthinkable Horror when my hearing started to come back.

The first thing I heard—and just barely—was Kevin squealing.

Kevin was upside down in one of the tentacles. S'wella was hanging desperately from one of his hooves.

I ran over, but they were lifted up beyond my reach. Then Chester was there. He cupped his

hands for me to step in and tried to launch me high
enough to grab S'wella's tail.

I fell back to the deck, hardly believing what was
happening. The sea witch had her big Ernie puppet
mouth open and was dangling nine or ten poten-
tial pirate meals over her mouth. She would hold
one over her mouth and smack her lips—like a little
cat playing with its food—and then move on to the
next.

I heard Ferlin behind me—letting out a groan
and a big burp as he came to—and suddenly I had
an idea. Ferlin's bag. The potions. It was a shot in
the dark, but it was a shot.

I took off running for the door to the cabins
below, threw it open, and pounded down the steps
four at a time. I ran into the bunkroom and straight

up to Ferlin's bunk . . . but his backpack wasn't there. My heart sank, until I heard a small sniffle near my feet.

I dropped to my hands and knees and saw the bag, clutched in Roquefort's stubby little fingers. He was tucked back under the bottom bunk, and he'd barricaded himself under there with pillows, blankets, and Ferlin's bag.

"I'd be out there defeating that thing if I wasn't singlehandedly the FUTURE of our KINGDOM."

There was a loud crash from above, and he looked up in terror.

I tried to grab the bag, but the prince wasn't letting go. Time was wasting, and I felt my troll anger kick back in. "Let go of the backpack, Roquefort. It might be our only chance."

The prince glared at me. "Well, I'm currently using it as a shield! So buzz off!"

That did it. Final straw. I yanked the bag out, with Roquefort still clinging to it, and took off for the stairs.

He bounced up a few stairs before he came to his senses and let go, fleeing back into the bunk-room.

I burst through the door and saw how badly the ship was leaning to one side. I realized we must be taking on water. I ran straight for the witch, who was still doing the cat-and-mouse thing with Kevin and the rest. It looked like Kevin was unconscious (as is his way), but S'wella had a good grip on him. Another tentacle reared up and I saw that the witch had Red and Chester now too.

Using every bit of troll strength I had, I smashed the backpack against the deck.

It sounded like an explosion of glass and liquid in there, just as I'd hoped. I reared back and held the bag out.

I kept going. "*I* TOOK THE BEANS! ISN'T THAT WHAT THIS IS ABOUT??"

Everything stopped. The tentacles stopped swaying, that big freaky mouth slammed shut, and those glowing red eyes turned in my direction.

I was starting to yell again when another tentacle came around from the back and caught me off guard, knocking the wind out of me. It slipped around my waist, and I gripped the backpack tightly as I was hauled into the air.

That nasty-looking face got closer and larger until I was dangling right in front of the witch's fuming eyes.

There was some serious, angry heat coming from them. I swallowed hard and kept goading her.

"YUM YUM YUM. Those beans were SCRUMPTIOUS!! I mean, these things were juicy and meaty and perfectly seasoned and . . ."

The mouth opened, and a rumbling voice that made my ears flutter started to roll out.

"MMMYYYY BEEEEEEEAAAAAAAA...."

I didn't wait. I chucked that dripping, oozing

backpack as hard as I could, right through those enormous greasy lips.

". . . AAAANNNNNSSSSSSSSSS!" The witch finished her word before she realized something had landed in her throat. Then she blinked and swallowed out of reflex. For a second, nothing moved.

The witch shook it off, almost like a kid on a bike who'd swallowed a fly.

Then it was back to business. The tentacle lifted me higher into the air until I was looking straight down on the witch. She let out a deep sound that sounded like a chuckle. That huge mouth started to open. And open. And open . . .

And then things started to happen.

First came a shudder—like an earthquake—that rumbled through the witch. She paused and lowered me just a bit, away from her mouth.

The shaking was growing stronger and stronger when her teeth started to fall out. They made splashes as each one hit the water—one or two at first, and then in groups of four or five at a time. There must have been some kind of anti-dental potion in that bag of tricks.

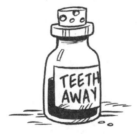

A gurgling came from the top of the witch's head. It was bubbling and squirming like a honey bog on a hot day, when there was a squishy bursting sound . . . and huge tufts of pink and purple hair started to explode out of her scalp. I mean huge shocks of hair, the size of the flumpfruit trees. One after another they unfolded and expanded until the witch's head was like a small forest.

Those horrible red eyes looked confused. She started shaking her enormous head, trying to figure out what was happening up there.

Then came the big changes.

A couple of huge bean leaves popped out of the tentacle wrapped around me, and I had a pretty good idea what was coming. More leaves started sprouting, and within a few seconds I was wrapped up in a loosening beanstalk. One by one I heard my friends plopping into the ocean as the beanstalks relaxed their grips and fell away.

As soon as I hit the water, I started swimming toward Kevin. Last I'd seen him, he was unconscious.

I swam over and under limp beanstalks and leaves, ignoring the cheers and pats on the back from the dogpaddling pirates around me.

There was a huge roar overhead as the sea witch rose up out of the water like a green big bowling pin in a disco wig.

The witch made a high-pitched squealing noise and fell slowly back away from us. As she fell, it looked like the potion combo was actually dissolving her in front of us—turning her skin to something like wet Kleenex. When she finally hit the water, she exploded. She split open like a piñata and mountains of multicolored magic beans burst out. Some flew into the sky and rained down, while others slid across the water amongst us and sank.

What the heck had Ferlin kept in that JanSport, anyway?

Treading water, I looked over at Chester, who was floating next to me.

S'wella swam up, supporting Kevin, who was still passed out. She hugged him cheek to cheek and let out a little Southern-tinged laugh.

·23·

LIMPING
HOME

SOGGY, BUT ALL MY IMPORTANT PARTS ARE STILL HERE.

Fifteen minutes later, everyone had climbed back on board and helped each other up the side of the leaning ship. We were a sorry-looking crew as we stood there dripping all over the deck.

MY KINGDOM FOR A BIG, FLUFFY TOWEL.

Kevin was waking up.

I started to laugh when someone grabbed me by the arm. Red gave me a huge hug. "You're either the bravest or luckiest troll I've ever met."

Red climbed up a few pegs on the side of the leaning mast. She had to yell over the wind, but everyone clammed up.

"You all have made me incredibly proud. You're the finest group of pirates a person could ask for, whether you're 'real' pirates or not."

Harry the bear sniffed loudly and blew his nose into a soaking wet handkerchief.

"We don't have a lot of time, because the ship is taking on water by the bucketful. But I have a daughter to see, and these brave kids have families that are worried sick about them."

She turned and looked at the gnome captain, leaning against a large barrel of deck wax. "Gerome, my friend, will you take us home?"

Gerome snapped to attention and saluted Red.

Without another word, the crew burst into activity. Sails were lowered and new ones went up in their place. Pirates flooded into the hull of the ship to stem the tide of incoming water. And within twenty minutes we were off. Damaged, slower, and a whole lot worse for wear—but we were moving again.

We sailed on for about an hour as the ship slowly got lower and more crooked in the water. Chester, Kevin, and I were part of a chain of people bringing full buckets of water up from the hull. I was dumping a large bucket over the side when Red grabbed my arm.

"Can you do something for me, Zarf?" She had a crooked smile on her face. I nodded, and she reached into her pocket. She handed me something in a ziplock bag. "We're close enough now."

I opened the bag and pulled out some kind of special sea phone in a red-and-black skull-and-crossbones case. The phone had a full signal. Four bars!

I laughed and started dialing my home phone. "With pleasure!"

While it rang, Red told me to let them know we'd be at the marina in about an hour. I was nodding my head when a familiar, gravelly voice picked up.

"Hello?"

I don't think I'd realized just how worried I'd been about him until that moment. A huge lump jumped up into my throat and tears shot into my eyes.

There was a split-second pause before he almost blew my eardrums out yelling to my parents. "IT'S HIM!! IT'S TH' BOY!! ZARF IS ON TH' RINGER!!"

We got so choked up we could barely make out what each other was saying as my parents scrambled and picked up the other lines, their shouting and crying adding to the confusion. It took some time, but I eventually got them calmed down enough to tell them what was happening.

"Wake up the Littlepigs and Mr. Flintwater! Have Goldie call Sierra and the king. Meet us at the docks!"

Forty-five minutes later I heard someone shout from the bow. "LAND HO!!"

Chester and I ran to the front of the ship and could just barely make out the lights of the harbor. Kevin, S'wella, and Red joined us while we quietly watched them grow closer.

The sky was turning amazing shades of purple and orange as the sun prepared to rise. When we were close enough to make out individual boats, I felt someone else step up beside me.

There wasn't, but as we pulled into the marina, the crowd was larger than I'd expected. Word must have spread.

The first person—or silhouette, really—I was able to pick out was Gramps. He was a big guy and hard to miss. As we slid up alongside the dock, he and my parents were front and center—my mom surrounded by a pile of used Kleenex.

The crew tied up the ship and we all crowded to get off. One of the female pirates was about to get off first until someone—I'll give you one guess who—started shoving his way through. Roquefort stepped up onto the short plank and yelled out to the king.

"This HORRIBLE troll and his FILTHY cohorts kidnapped me and tried to FORCE me into who knows . . ." His words died off as King Cheznott stepped in front of him. The king's face was anything but warm and welcoming.

"Can it, Roquefort." He spoke loud enough that everyone could hear. "I've had some long talks with Mr. Belford over there"—he pointed at Gramps—"and I know the score."

Roquefort's face dropped and he began sputtering. "But . . . but I've been through such HARD-SHIPS, Father!"

King Cheznott grabbed Roquefort by the ear and led him off the plank.

They made their way through the stunned crowd, the sound of Roquefort's sniveling slowly fading away.

Sierra stepped forward. Despite a decent case of bed head, she looked great. She appeared happy and confused at the same time.

I stepped through the crowd and walked up to her. She gave me a hug and told me how glad she was that I was okay. I couldn't stop smiling, knowing what was coming.

I stepped out of the way and looked back. Harry and a few others stepped back to let Red walk down the plank. She had her eyes down until she was a few steps from Sierra. When she looked up, she was nervously chewing on her lip—the way I'd seen Sierra do about a million times before.

HI, SIERRA.
I'M HOME.

Sierra gasped as the crowd on the dock burst into some major murmuring—Red Ridinghood was a bit of a celebrity, after all. Sierra stood there for a few moments like she didn't trust her eyes. I was starting to think she was frozen when she let out a sob and ran into her mom's arms.

Okay, look. I know this is getting a little mushy, but it was a *seriously* touching moment. You'd have to be a robot to not get misty watching this.

Everyone swept in at that point. My family. The Littlepigs, Goldie. The Knoble Knight. Chester's dad. Harbormaster Sprat.

It was a regular HugFest, and there wasn't a dry eye on that dock by the time all of the Welcome Homes were done.

· 24 ·

GOOD OL'
COTSWIN

Kevin didn't come by the house before school
the next morning, but he sent me a text telling
me where he'd be. I had to leave a little early to
make it down to the harbor in time to get him.

I found him sitting by himself at the end of a dock.

Kevin looked up at me with a sad smile on his face. "Hey Z. She just took off. We agreed to meet down here this morning."

He got up and we looked out at the water for a couple of minutes. A goat puttered by in a tugboat and gave us a quick wave.

We turned and headed for school, and I gave him a pat on the back. "Got it bad, huh buddy?"

Kevin let out a long sigh.

I really didn't, but I decided to keep that to myself. We were coming up the hill when we met up with Chester.

"Turning over a new leaf today, gentlemen! I've got a new comedic outlook."

"I told my dad all about my new storytelling thing and he's stoked! Thinks maybe I oughta start a podcast!"

Right before we reached the doors of the school, Sierra came running out and gave me another hug. (Not a bad way to start a school day, I have to say.)

She was grinning ear to ear. "We stayed up all night talking and catching up. Thank you, Zarf. Again." I'm pretty sure I blushed, though hopefully my fur hid it. Sierra grabbed my arm. "And oh, buh-rother. Can I just tell you how my mom won't shut up about you?"

We all walked in the front door together, and hadn't even made it out of the foyer when everyone's favorite goat, Sten Vinders, started in.

I'd barely had time to react before Sierra spun around to face him.

"Get bent, Sten. You wanna talk about stink? You eat garbage for lunch and smell like a petting zoo."

I couldn't believe it. Sten's face and shoulders fell before he slumped off into the bathroom with his tail between his legs.

Sierra looked back at me. "I know that was mean, but he started it."

I wasn't complaining.

We split up as we went to our lockers. I was finishing my combo when Rebb Glumfort ran up and slammed into the locker next to me.

"Zarf!!" He was out of breath. "How are you feeling? I heard you ate some of those magic beans."

I'D FEEL EVER SO GUILTY IF YOU SUFFERED ADVERSE EFFECTS DUE TO MY CARELESS RECOMMENDATIONS.

(Seriously. He talks like that.)

I smiled and pulled out a couple of textbooks. "I'm fine, Rebb. I turned into a potted plant for a while, but it's all good now."

Rebb's shoulders relaxed. "Oh, thank Merlin's ghost. I was ever so concerned."

I closed my locker and started walking with him. "But, Rebb . . . I am curious. Did you know when you told Roquefort? That they wouldn't work right?"

Rebb's eyes got shifty, and a hint of a smile slid over his face.

I'M AFRAID I SHOULD PLEAD THE FIFTH, LEST I UNDULY INCRIMINATE MYSELF.

Whatever that means. Then he slid off into the crowded hallway.

When the bell rang, we were all in our seats with the exception of Roquefort. Miss Flett blew into the room and began class without seeming to notice. Or maybe she knew something.

Then, about fifteen minutes in, Principal Haggard came over the PA system and asked for Kevin and Chester and me to come to the office.

NOTHING BAD, GUYS. DON'T FREAK OUT.

Kevin still freaked out a little.

We got to the office to find the king and Roquefort

standing there with Principal Haggard. Roquefort was looking at the floor, the ceiling—anywhere but at us.

Principal Haggard led us all into his office and closed the door. We stood there awkwardly until the king cleared his throat. He smiled at each of us in turn. "My son has something he wishes to say."

Nobody said anything until the king swatted Roquefort on the arm.

Roquefort looked up for about a split second and then barely spoke.

"Sorry."

The king rolled his eyes. "What was that, young man? Speak up."

FINE! WHATEVER! I'M SORRY I DID STUFF AND YOU IDIOTS WENT ALONG WITH IT!

The king sighed and rubbed the bridge of his nose. "Sadly, that may be the best we'll get today, gentlemen. But I can assure you there will be more—better—apologies coming. Like the one we're about to go deliver to Zarf's grandfather. Right, son?"

Roquefort was dying. "Whatever, Dad!!"

With that, the king and the unruly prince left and closed the door behind them.

SWEET MOTHER OF PEARL! DID THAT REALLY JUST HAPPEN?

Principal Haggard laughed and plopped down in his chair.

CAN I TELL YOU HOW MUCH YOU ALL EXHAUST ME?

PRINCIPAL HAGGARD

He went on. "But Goldie wanted me to let you know she has a fresh batch of mutton muffins—just out of the oven—with your names on them. So I'm excusing you for the rest of this period. Head down there. I'm pretty certain you've earned it."

Chester and I thanked him, but Kevin was already heading for the door in a zombie mutton trance. He may have been drooling a little, to be honest.

So we went to the cafeteria, where Goldie really did have mutton muffins with our names on them in cream cheese icing.

Best muffin I ever had.

THE END

ABOUT
THE AUTHOR

Rob Harrell created and drew the internationally syndicated comic strip *Big Top*, as well as the acclaimed graphic novel *Monster on the Hill*. He also writes and draws the long-running daily comic strip *Adam@Home*. He survived middle school and now lives with his wife in Indianapolis, Indiana. Visit his website at www.lifeofzarf.com.